Barbara Romanik, J.M. Villaverde & Jasmina Odor

COMING ATTRACTIONS
05

We acknowledge the support of the Canada Council for the Arts, the Government of Ontario through the Ontario Media Development Corporation and the Government of Canada through the Book Publishing Industry Development ment Program for our publishing activities.

"A Creator Who Cares About You" by Barbara Romanik and "Dance of the Suitors" and "Tatyana's House" by J.M. Villaverde first appeared in *The Fiddlehead.*

ISBN 0 7780 1271 9 (hardcover)
ISBN 0 7780 1272 7 (softcover)

Cover art by Paul Signac
Book design by Michael Macklem

Printed in Canada

PUBLISHED IN CANADA BY OBERON PRESS

Contents

INTRODUCTION

Here are nine stories that piece the heart, pierce the eye.

Barb Romanik makes me care (somehow!) about a mechanical teddy bear who goes door-to-door for the Jehovah's Witnesses and is almost murdered by coffee poured down his throat, à la Hamlet and Claudius. Her writing is delightful, weird, unpredictable, dream-like, yet utterly convincing. The stories are incredibly diverse: she can write with verve about Poland, India, Italy and English football stadiums.

Joe Villaverde dishes up gem-like insights and casual bon-mots in beautiful prose that is striking and mysteriously assertive, brimming with whimsy and darkness. His stories examine the minute flashpoints of a life and a family, hurly burly moments in schoolbuses and on basement couches, strange revelations where God is in the candid ice-cool details.

Jasmina Odor writes wryly of different generations and cultures and the wider perspectives of the immigrant experience, displaying a maturity beyond her years, a talent and vision I admire. Jasmina Odor's prose is calm, yet unsettling at the same time, a palimpsest. She shuns sentiment and hyperbole, but instills an uncanny blend of puzzlement and pathos and humour.

Three young writers worth watching, three golden guides spinning sensual tales of great pith and moment, tales of travel and travail, tales of flowering frustrations and stellar loves.

MARK ANTHONY JARMAN

Contributions for Coming Attractions 06, *published or unpub-lished, should be sent to Oberon Press, 205—145 Spruce Street, Ottawa, Ontario KIR 6PI before 31 March, 2006. All manu-scripts should enclose a stamped self-addressed envelope.*

BARBARA ROMANIK

A Creator Who Cares About You

"...The career path you weren't on is opening before you, whoever might win the election." Teddy reads his horoscope, perplexed. In order to see out of the car's front windshield, he's sitting up on the stack of *Watchtowers*.

We're addicted to bad astrology.

"What's my horoscope, Teddy?"

"Because your favourite football player is traded to a team you've always despised, your life will spiral out of control. Also, it looks like you will marry a woman you don't love."

"What?! Well, she's going to have to get in line behind the woman who feels sorry for me."

"Fine Print." Teddy points to the column with his paw and starts to fold the paper. "Keep your eyes on the road," he tells me. Compared to Teddy, the newsprint is HUGE. With its parachute risk of entanglements, I worry. I snerk a look out of the corner of my eye.

Three feet tall, Teddy's furry, stuffed and lovable: a robotic super-toy bear. There's no way in hell he's getting into heaven, but this has not curbed Teddy's zeal. Despite my shortcomings, Teddy's schooling me in the ways of Jehovah.

The first bungalow door is opened by a man in his hockey pyjamas and a bathrobe. He stares at me severely holding onto a coffee mug like he and the mug are about to be cannon-balled out into space. What Teddy and I don't know at that moment is that we would be lucky if this man was just another stay-at-home husband, classically sailing the Odyssean sea of middle-aged baldness toward alcoholism. Instead, he is one deranged motherfucker named Cliff J. Eastwoof.

"Hello, we are visiting with our neighbours today. Some of them believe that there is a God but others don't. How do you feel about it? Would you like to talk to us about the Creator for a little bit? My name is Randal." I lean casually forward and place my foot inside of the door.

The man reluctantly shakes my hand, introduces himself and zeroes in on Teddy with a curious (or what I later realize to have been pathologically hateful) look.

"Guess I have nothing better to do..." he says bitterly.

I pick up my bear pal, smile at him, and enter. We don't usually get invited inside without haggling. But like old whores, we remain eternally optimistic.

Walking into a stranger's house, all of the man's junk in the hallways, makes me think of my own home and why I have taken a day off per week to do this in the first place. My wife, Alise, is a Jehovah's Witness and beautiful enough to destroy any man, but she's also paralyzed from her waist down. None of the treatments and surgeries had worked and we have given up hope she'll ever be able to walk. In a moment of weakness, compassion or something like charity I volunteered to spread Jehovah's teachings. It's been close to six months since I started.

Last week, over cornflakes, Alise told me that two days from now she will undergo an experimental procedure that will either allow her to walk again or kill her.

I look at the Bible in my hands. Teddy and I have aid. We're armed with booklets such as *The Watchtower* and my personal favourite *Is there a Creator who cares about you?* Teddy whispers into my ear to relax. I'm trying to decide between Psalm 19 and a passage from the *Creator* as I sit Teddy down on the couch beside me.

Cliff asks, "So how long have you, bear, been Jehoving?"

"I'm Teddy," Teddy answers. "My work in the ministry of spreading the good news began four years ago with my first family who were Jehovah's Witnesses." He proceeds to explain that the father, one Germaine Dobson, would bring Teddy along with him on his door to door wanderings. Cliff smiles and tightens his grip on the half-empty coffee cup.

I try charging into Creator's business with "Scientists deny that the universe was created by a higher intelligence yet they expect...."

But Eastwoof ignores me completely. "And you are no longer with that family?" he asks Teddy.

"No," Teddy tells him, "Dizzy, Monique and Clarence are too old for toys now. I was going to be recycled so I called up our local chapter of the Jehovah's Witnesses, explained my dedication to Jehovah and offered my services to them. Long story short, here I am—," Teddy says.

We all laugh, a strained salesman laugh.

"I used to be a paper mill foreman," the man tells us. "Part of my job was taking care of programming the machines that did all the manual work. That was until I was made redundant by them. And replaced. Replaced by computers that become obsolete and useless every year or two. Machines just like you," he tells Teddy.

I know now we won't be getting to the Creator for awhile, but I'm still dumb, smiling. "When I started university, I was out of a summer job," I say. "They had gotten these shapely looking bots to dispense cotton candy at the amusement park, where I worked since I was fifteen." Cliff looks at me furiously but I don't let it faze me, I have a point. "We're in the clutches of the computer age and have difficulty seeing beyond it. But we all know that even most advanced computers are primitive compared to the human brain with its 50 billion neutrons, a million billion synapses, and overall firing rate of 10 million billion times per second...."

Eastwoof's on his own trip and won't have any of it. "Our government cares less for the rights of its people than for fucking machines. It's cheaper for them to replace us. It's us who are dispensable!"

Hard to argue with the truth, but I make a valiant attempt at a bypass. "Which brings us to the question, if man were merely an accidental grouping of nucleic acid and protein molecules, why would those molecules develop a love of art and beauty, turn religious and contemplate eternity? Could it be because there is a God?"

I seem to have a singular gift for enraging people in volatile situations. I can't pick up any cues from Teddy because he's sitting possum having decided that his silence might be our best bet.

Cliff goes on ranting, staring at Teddy, gesticulating with his arms about how he's been out of work for two and a half years and all because of machines like Teddy.

I suggest that perhaps Teddy and I should leave. It is when I distractedly raise myself up from his couch that Cliff seizes Teddy. With amazing speed, for a couch potato, he pours the remainder of his coffee down Teddy's little mouth. I grab the bear and make a dash right out of the house. When I'm inside the car, I realize Cliff has not followed us outside. Still I drive off, spooked.

Teddy's not doing so well beside me in the passenger seat; his eyes are rolling like marbles in his furry head and the right side of his body, his arm, leg and paws are twitching uncontrollably. An electric sizzling noise is rising deep out of his body. In a broken voice he is repeating, "Ta-ke me to As-ha Du-dor...."

"Maybe a repair shop, why Asha's?" I ask, panicked.

"Asha, A-sha, A-sss-ha...."

"All right," I finally agree. Asha is one of the regulars Teddy visited in his early days with Germaine Dobson. He has taken me to visit her once or twice so I could practice my "Jehoving" on her. After fifteen minutes of my clumsy attempts to quote the material I had memorized, Asha took me and Teddy out to her garden and handed me a glass of brandy. I remember admiring her garden. It was surrounded with an eight-foot-tall wall, escaping most of the city's noise. Surprisingly her property, so close to the city's centre, hadn't been bought out by some large company or the city itself.

Asha herself is in her late seventies. Not old by today's standards, but strangely antique in her mannerisms and wardrobe. Her long grey hair rests in a bun on top of her head and she wears overalls and cotton shirts. Unlike some older women, her features have not softened or sharpened in old age, no round child-like cheeks or a spectacularly beaked nose. Just sunbrown skin of an expert gardener. And an air of a capable woman, certainly more capable of taking care of Teddy than I am.

"As-ha," Teddy sputters upon seeing Asha. All his systems go off.

"What happened?" Asha asks.

"Someone poured coffee down his mouth."

Asha looks up at me quizzically. She picks Teddy up in her arms with the softness and attention a mother might pick up a child, a husband his bride. "My laboratory is in the garden shed; I should be able to fix and clean him up within an hour or two," she says. I follow her to the shed, thinking I might be of help but once I see her equipment, the intricate computer parts I could never name, and her mechanical assistants, I give up and go sit in the garden to wait.

She calls me when she is nearly finished. I watch as she smoothes down Teddy's right leg. Softly, hooking the middle finger beneath his knee, she presses lightly. The intimacy of the gesture embarrasses me. Then Asha closes Teddy's front and pats him there.

Teddy sits up and looks around at both me and Asha and I have to laugh at the almost surprised expression on his face.

"Sorry for not having your back there, pal. Didn't know what to do."

"No problem," Teddy says, "You did fine."

I place my hand on Teddy's head and let it rest there for a second.

But all is fair with the world and Teddy is loosed on Asha's beautiful garden once more.

Asha and I should have horrible qualms when we watch his brown ears as he's flickering between the lady's delight and the white bleeding heart bush. Teddy walks with the gait of a man but runs the way a child might, stilted and quick. Makes me think of a child. What does Asha, sitting beside me, think—I can't tell. Maybe she sees herself a flawed creator, whose love is none the worse for wear, creating wonder—here in the garden—the flowers and Teddy's exuberance. His brown body weaves through the greenery and baby's breath and then he gets on his paws and knees to thread among the violets, sniffing at the flowers he cannot smell. His right ear perks up and he goes off chasing a white cabbage butterfly.... I'm about to chase after him when I feel Asha grab my arm with a strength of a horse. "I couldn't help myself," she confesses. "With the alterations I've made to him over the years, Teddy's not simply another super toy...." I nod hoping this will shut her up. Prevent her from saying another word, implicating me. The terror in my face must be evident for she lets me go, doesn't even laugh or smile, just dismisses me. She's unable to confide, unable to find release from her responsibilities. And I follow Teddy among the azaleas and we chase each other around the garden like teenagers. Our lightheartedness borders on hysterical.

Asha's Dream: A large house, long hallway with arches, exquisitely tiled floor, no bedrooms, long galleries and ballrooms. Young, in her thin tan coat, she's following a group of three older men in black suits. They defer to her in a charming, bored way, smoking and pointing, the way they might do if they were touring around someone's daughter or a girlfriend, a pretty stranger. She follows one of the men into a lounge-like room with a TV, a black table and a green modern couch. She sits on the edge of her side of the couch while the man lounges on the other. They are watching a male comedy duo on the TV, Dean Martin and Jerry Lewis. Physical comedy: old-fashioned sparring on black and white screen, Asha doesn't get it. The man laughs; her eyes linger on him. They exchange looks and he continues to laugh, repeats the last punchline to her in an amused way. When she laughs softly but does not look back to the screen, he puts his drink on the table in front of them and lets her take a good look at him. The way his arms spread on the couch, he leaves himself open up to her scrutiny: every blemish and wrinkle in his skin— his shirt is open at his neck, his tie crooked. In his late fifties, he continues to age well, without sobriety. What Asha feels for this man is desire, unadulterated by love, guilt or respect, just desire. In this room, perhaps beyond all rooms, Asha does not want love. She wants an equal sign. Give equals take, with this man the scale balances. And she nears him on the green couch, feels its plush felt, the fabric of her dress beneath her coat. Closer, feels the stiffness fading out of his collar with her hands upon it, her knee between his legs. And because this time the dream does not end here, because Asha doesn't wake up, she smiles softly biting his lip. Asha knows she is dying.

Sitting diagonally on the bed and leaning against the wall, I look out of ours, Alise's and my, second-storey window. From a height, the highway lights leading into the city appear connected, strung-up rows of Christmas strings. When we first moved in five years ago, we made love to their highway-strung nightly consistency. We appeared fearless in the dark, Alise and I. Perhaps we mistook ourselves for pilots of planes that criss-cross above the metropolis, seeing the world in a fast, red impulse. Getting seduced by black river tongues snaking below, we could've stood up buildings like matches. And the trains. We would always hear them in the night and in the morning but could never remember hearing any during the day. Now I fall asleep with them at 2.30 in the morning and wake with them around 7 AM.

Our suburb, along others, besieges the city at its limits.

Train tracks lead to the city core. Uphill our neighbourhood climbs in the opposite direction. You can't feel the steady incline in the car or when walking but try riding a bicycle up our street and you'll feel a shortness of breath. I've often wondered if someone could mistake that shortness of breath for love. A silly girl might: riding her bicycle to see a boy, she might think the shortness and cramps in her belly had nothing to do with the steepness of the incline and the laws of gravity. Love, she might think. Maybe the heat would compound her confusion and she'd find herself light-headed until yellow spots started appearing in her vision and she'd lose her balance and swerve into oncoming traffic. And then would wake, up to her waist, underneath the body of a car.

A month after she was able to walk again, Alise packed one suitcase and left. She said I was worse than a 2500 pound car. Pinning her down. But I couldn't get used to her legs, moving beneath me. I had never made love to her before the accident and it felt obscene like there was someone else in bed with us.

She claimed I wanted her to play dead. She said a great many things and I responded with many other things, which out of context can only be silly but in the space of two weeks meant the breaking of something that seemed cemented and unbreakable for five years.

I hear someone standing in the door. I have a fright before I realize it's Teddy.

"How'd you get in?"

"The door was open."

"Shit."

"Didn't meant to startle. I wasn't going to wake you if you were sleeping."

"What would you have done if I was sleeping?"

"I'd wait on your porch until a more reasonable hour and ring the doorbell."

Teddy offers me his arm and I lift him onto the bed. He settles himself beside me looking toward the lights.

"What's in the charts Teddy? What's in the stars?"

"Dark ages ahead. Asha's dead."

"Um, no." I make a guttural, lame-ass sort of sound that couldn't even satisfy a super-toy bear. But Teddy does not call me on it. We spoke last a month ago when I told him Alise left me and I wouldn't be Jehoving anymore. At the time, he mentioned that Asha was in the hospital and might appreciate a visit from me. I didn't go.

"She left me everything."

"What?"

"Her house and garden, all her money. She left me everything providing I find myself a human guardian."

"Oh." I turn to the window wondering what Teddy makes of these lights, all of this. More signs of a higher intelligence, design, meaning?

"Thinking about your wife?" he asks.

"Um."

Teddy places his right paw between my legs. "I can help."

I look down, shake my head. "Keep your paws to yourself, you perverted robot." I try to muster rage and indignation but can't.

Teddy takes his paw back and we sit quietly as the lights shiver in the night.

"May I tell you something?" Teddy finally breaks the silence.

"Sure, shoot."

"You have to first promise that you'll still be my guardian."

I nod my head, place my right hand on my heart but pull my left arm behind my back and cross my fingers. "Whatever you tell me Teddy, I'll still be your guardian."

"One, you don't love your wife. Two, you're a homosexual. And three, you don't believe in Jehovah—so you won't share in the heavenly Kingdom with Christ."

"Um. Anything else, Sherlock?"

"No." Teddy turns to face me. "Now can we go over to Asha's house? I want to wake up from my first dream in her garden. And a drink of her pear brandy might do wonders for your disposition."

"But you don't sleep or dream."

"Before Asha's death she gave me a final gift, a program for dreaming."

"Why didn't she give me one?"

Teddy shrugs. "Maybe because you don't need one."

"Oh." I scratch Teddy's head and he blinks slowly.

In Asha's garden there is no sign that Asha has died; everything seems to be keeping quite well. True, it has only been a week. Perhaps someone familiar with gardens would know better, perhaps even Teddy knows where neglect is creeping in. I hold a bottle of brandy and sing to myself softly. Lovely voice if I say so myself; I was in a boys' choir until I hit puberty. Teddy sits on his Bible in the grass and watches the stars. He has built himself a bit of a shelter off the patio for protection from the elements. At least for tonight, he wants to sleep outside. I don't want to ruin Teddy's enthusiasm by telling him dreams are nothing worth having. The night is beautiful and I can't imagine rain falling onto our drunkenness. There is clematis climbing up the patio railings and bell-full delphiniums growing tall. Peonies, hollyhocks and sweet peas are about to bloom and it's enough to make a grown man weep and I do. It's looking up at the stars, which should be obscured and dead in the middle of the city, but are not. Asha's here in spirit. I stop singing and just listen to the insects and the night.

Teddy's dream: Teddy enters the garden and the irises, Asha's favourite flowers, are in bloom. A dark, heavy black purple called black dragon *sticks out his black beard at Teddy. It leans forward as if mouthing something, the way bearded irises tend to do. Horizontal standards and falls, pendant-huge, beckon. Teddy raises his arms and takes the blooming flower in his paws the way he has inspected Asha's flowers before. Watching for change in colour and shape of the petal; lightly fingering the spreading crest. But something feels different about the flower. He holds it for a long time in his paws until he realizes he can smell it. He twitches his nose and he smells a sweetness; by all description this is what sweetness*

19

smells like. Teddy smiles. From there on he goes to a Piccadilly rose; here the scent is lighter but more acerbic. Teddy hugs the flower to himself, thinks if he's lucky the thorns may sting and he will bleed. Or better yet, he may never wake up.

Caught Up

"Hey Johnny Rotten, what's up with the do?" I ask as my girlfriend's hair gives me the finger first thing in the morning.

"I fell asleep with wet hair."

"Can't you flatten it down with water or gel?"

"Gel?" Bea frowns as if I had suggested nuclear fusion.

I scratch my ass, stumped. "Well did you try brushing it?"

"Fuck you." Obviously the hair has taken over.

I know better than to comment on her outfit.

Because of "the hair" we are late for the bus. Even though my girlfriend shifts gears and sprints after the bus, the driver doesn't stop! "Fuck you, you bastard," she screams enraged, taking in oxygen, fast. Then she throws a fit the likes of which I have never seen. "Kurwa mac, popierdolony swiecie. Popierdolony, pojebany, skorwielcowy swiecie tylko chcialam herbaty, cholera jasna." None of this speaking in foreign tongues matters because I know she is only avoiding the real culprit, which is of course "the hair" (no longer her hair but an entity of its own). She even takes off her toque, stomps on it and kicks it into the ditch, forsaking the usual unhealthy commitment she makes to each piece of clothing she owns. When I make a move to retrieve the toque, Bea yells *Dotknij, a zginiesz!*" Death threats don't need a universal translator.

Watching someone throw a fit gets pretty old, as a spectator sport, unless you're actively participating in making a scene and embarrassing yourself. We decide to walk it. The fifteen-minute walk will take us down 66th Street to the No. 10 bus stop. Catching that bus will make us fifteen minutes late rather than the 30 minutes we would be if we waited for our regular bus to come again. We are meeting my father for brunch. Just the idea of this makes me queasy.

I have been a hit with Beata's *foreignese* parents on an occasion or two. I'm not quite sure whether it is a case of low standards or pure relief; whichever it is, it should not be frowned upon. My parents are a different story all together. Divorced and not better for it, they are nitpickers and hate everything inside and outside of themselves. This "brunching" with my father makes me worried for myself, my girlfriend, and by some law of inclusion "the hair."

"I wish that bus crashes and the bus driver and everyone aboard it goes to hell!"

I look at her doubtfully. My girl is a spy from parts unknown. Sometimes she slips up and says something like "where I was born they have statues of poets like here they have of explorers" it doesn't help that being a (co)lapsed catholic she is harassed by God on a regular basis and tormented by our blasphemous worship of the game. I'm pretty sure the only reason we're still together is that on our own we couldn't afford the cable payments and Saturday mornings of Barclay Premiership Football.

"I wish hell on everything and everyone." Upon this, my girlfriend folds her anger into a tight envelope around herself ready to burst open again any minute. Her silence isn't much better, but it saves energy.

Because I refused to speak about God, Bea tried to prove to me the worthiness of suffering on earth by producing a cheap *Woodmerit* edition of *Hamlet*. "Look," she pointed out, "this goodly frame the earth seems to me a sterile purgatory; this most excellent canopy, the air...." I think she was trying to say that Shakespeare knew about purgatory on earth, but I grabbed the book from her. "What? Let me take a look. I think that's supposed to be promontory not purgatory. It's just a spelling mistake. Happens in these cheap editions." Bea looked at me with incomprehension and shock. She threw the book straight out of our three-storey window.

We tramp onto the bus and sit down. Obscenely flamboyant, "the hair" doesn't let up. It bends, folds and sticks out in all different directions. Bea glares at me when she catches the horror on my face as I observe "the hair." Finally I spit into both of my hands, place them on Bea's head, and smooth her hair down. I sacrifice my Arsenal toque to pacify the hair; I place it and pull it down over my girlfriend's head and around her ears. She shakes her head.

The bus, frustrated, manoeuvres the snow-blocked residential streets. Its wheels lumber through our northeastern, grey-ridden corner of suburbia, lapsing briefly into slumburbia. It's there the caterpillar bus raises its nose at the white trash and arrives at the above ground subway station of Coliseum. After we get on the train, it takes five minutes to leave the dirt and wiggle underground. Five minutes later, we slide into the belly of Edmonton's downtown.

The Other Belly of the Beast otherwise known as Inferno
Otherwise Known As: Hillsborough Stadium
Club: Sheffield Wednesday FC
Capacity: 39,900 seats (after 15 April, 1989)
Record Attendance: 72,841, Sheffield Wednesday-Manchester City; 1934
How to get there?
By Bus: line 53, 77 & 80 (from Flat Street), line 74 & 74a (from Angel Street) or line 85 & 86 (from Snig Hill).
By Supertram: Take the South Yorkshire Supertram toward Middlewood Road (yellow route). Exit at Leppings Lane.
The Prices:
South Stand: £21.00
North Stand: £18.00
Kop: £15.00
Depending upon your seat, the prices vary. The West Stand tickets are reserved for special 'away' supporters.

I re-examine the menu.

"You have an accent, don't you?" This is the fifth wrong question my father asks Bea. She nods. She hates my father immediately and completely and one day he'll grow on her but today is not that day. My father is trying on his crass American. If my father is a blood-sucking capitalist, with a fake Texan accent, I'm an anglophile. I think British punk was real and today's punk is just pretty. And I have links of holy trinities like The Clash, Sex Pistols and Joy Division and more recently Radiohead, Massive Attack, Portishead. Mostly I think the British came out of a pocket much neater than other creatures and Winston Churchill, Margaret Thatcher and Tony Blair frighten me spectacularly. I think they're mechanical dolls: alive, out of control, with flaming tongues. Fascinating. I think Malcolm McDowell, Hugh Laurie.... Well, I buy British, music mostly, and their football memorabilia, at expensive imported prices.

My father admittedly has an amazing insight into American pop culture and music. At 39, when he asked my mom for a divorce, he was listening to Smashing Pumpkins and Pavement. There are countless other bands my father has ruined for me by distilling their music. He's a cultural parasite, an entertainment lawyer.

"I'm not sure I understand. You work for a company that hires musicians to play at various public and private functions and buys rights to lyrics and music for various ad campaigns?" Bea asks my father, spreading butter on her bun. Her little finger is carefully up in the air separated from its companions.

"That's how I explain it to my moronic son. Ha, ha, ha." My father laughs and slaps my shoulder.

Bea nods not looking up from her plate.

"Hey!" I defend myself.

"What's your bra size B24/26?" my father asks.

My girlfriend looks up.

"Maybe I could pick you up something, next time I go to New York. Sometimes it helps out if a man buys a girl something nice to wear. Something a little sexy...."

Bea stares at my father. Oh, she hates him good.

"That reminds me," my father continues on obliviously, "that sexy girl that you used to date, Susan?"

"Zuzana."

"Yeah her, with the pink hair and that tattoo on her back, beautiful. You don't have a tattoo, do you?" He turns to Bea.

"No." She says this flatly, kind of smiling, kind of not. It's really hard to tell if she's still trying or if she has given up.

"What happened?" My father turns away from my girlfriend and speaks to me. "Didn't she sing in a band? Kind of punk? She was really hot."

"I killed her and buried her under Mom's house."

Safety First: The Taylor Report

Standing terraces in England were phased out in 1989 after Justice Taylor's report into the events of the Hillsborough disaster at the Sheffield Wednesday Football ground on 15 April, 1989. During an FA Cup semi-final match between Liverpool and Nottingham Forest 96 Liverpool fans were killed because of over-crowding.

This incident was due to congestion. Thousands of fans travelling to the game were late because of the traffic delays on the roads and the railway. However, nobody at the football ground thought it appropriate to delay the 3 PM kick off time. Many fans hurriedly entered the ground at the same time to avoid missing any further action. Furthermore, no effort was made to relieve the overcrowding: no entrances were sealed off and none of the fans were redirected to safer areas. The ineffectiveness and slowness of the police in reacting to the disaster contributed to the deaths.

The Taylor Report recommended that all top division stadiums in England and Scotland phase out their concrete terraces and become all-seater venues. As a result of this report, every top club, in both countries, has spent millions of pounds on rebuilding their grounds. While many fans have complained that the elimination of the standing terraces has ruined the atmosphere at football matches, all-seater stadiums are far safer to manage if each ticket is sold for a specific seat.

The inquiry, which was held in Sheffield, began on 15 May, 1989 and lasted 31 days.

"Your dad didn't like me."

"It was probably...'the hair.'"

"Shut the fuck up about the hair," Bea raises her voice. Then she bites her lip and pulls my toque over her eyes. She reminds me of the spinach-crazed Popeye as she marches down Jasper Ave.

What can I do—my parents still get deep between my skin and nails.

We walk together, not speaking. We try to get out of the way of downtowners. Our minimum wage resistance to the genteel drudgery of white collar is now only a front. We secretly hope one of us is smart enough or brave enough to sell out. I look to the city for clues.

At its best, downtown circles into suburbia, slumburbia, all of them; it's not too ashamed to stroke the sides of richville, sky-tall apartments, and the wannabe millionburbia hugging the river. At its worst, downtown lets itself go east of 97th Street. It turns into crumbling concrete, broken glass and rotted plywood of buildings, parking-lots, and street alleys behind the restaurants, bars and the sex-shops. There the pavement gives birth to resignation, a numbing stench of nuclear proportions, as mouldy as cheese and just as deadly. Yet both Little Italy and Chinatown manage to rise to the top of it like cream. The wind and the snow, winter's avenging angels, have covered most of it up and masked the stale odour.

With the sunshine, twelve degrees below is pleasant relief. We need comfort. At the Bay station, we get back on the subway and head back north toward the Stadium.

Bea was born in a city of God, Catholic Renaissance church God. Not as erect as High Gothic but not the triangular verging on squarish of modern, North American churches either. I've seen her photos of domed churches. Domes that compromise steeples with their roundness but won't dizzy you with possibilities. While to me they are just brick, concrete and wood, you could say, churches get my girl off.

On the train I say, "Last night I dreamt I met you in a crowded bar and you were wearing an *I love Tony Adams* T-shirt. Your hair was something awful."

My girl smiles. She says, "And this was funny because— you were also wearing an *I love Tony Adams* T-shirt?"

"Yes, yes I was. But funny? Hell no. I said to you, 'Nobody loves Tony Adams the way I love Tony Adams!' In the dream, you gulped down some beer, sized me up, and said to me with scorn, 'Prove it.' And I was indignant: 'If Tony Adams was here I would get down on my knees, take a hold of those tight buttocks, unzip his fly with my teeth, and get on with business.' Then you tapped the shoulder of the man that was sitting on a bar stool facing the bar and asked, 'So whattaya think, Tony?' And it was Tony Adams in a sexy black T. Turning around he said, 'Sounds like love to me.'"

My girl says, "Wow."

I ignore her. "Yes. It was you, me and Tony Adams and every possible position known to human kind and a couple Tony must have invented just for us." I punctuate my words with profuse nods. Smiling, I include the neatly dressed elderly man in the seat across from us. He's been pretending he hasn't been listening since Churchill Station. And maybe he hasn't. "I bet Tony Adams could teach us all a thing or two."

"Um." My girlfriend nods. "Now that his drunk-driving

27

days are over." She makes fun but she doesn't really mean it. Painfully and crudely, what my girl prizes in a footballer, above all skill, is heart and guts. And Tony wears those well.

We come above ground two blocks from Stadium and faded graffiti salutes us from both sides of the tracks as we speed toward our destination. Someone must have time on their hands, I think.

promontory **graffiti**
John Alfred Anderson (62) Colin Mark Ashcroft (19)
James Gary Aspinall (18) Kester Roger Marcus Ball (16)
Gerard Bernard Patrick Baron (67) Simon Bell (17)
Barry Sidney Bennett (26) David John Benson (22)
David William Birtle (22) Tony Bland (22) Paul David
Brady (21) Andrew Mark Brookes (26) Carl Brown (18)
David Steven Brown (25) Henry Thomas Burke (47)
Peter Andrew Burkett (24) Paul William Carlile (19)
Raymond Thomas Chapman (50) Gary Christopher
Church (19) Joseph Clark (29) Paul Clark (18) Gary
Collins (22) Stephen Paul Copoc (20) Tracey Elizabeth
Cox (23) James Philip Delaney (19) Christopher Barry
Devonside (18) Christopher Edwards (29) Vincent
Michael Fitzsimmons (34) Thomas Steven Fox (21) Jon-
Paul Gilhooley (10) Barry Glover (27) Ian Thomas
Glover (20) Derrick George Godwin (24) Roy Harry
Hamilton (34) Philip Hammond (14) Eric Hankin (33)
Gary Harrison (27) Stephen Francis Harrison (31) Peter
Andrew Harrison (15) David Hawley (39) James Robert
Hennessy (29) Paul Anthony Hewitson (26) Carl Darren
Hewitt (17) Nicholas Michael Hewitt (16) Sarah Louise
Hicks (19) Victoria Jane Hicks (15) Gordon Rodney
Horn (20) Arthur Horrocks (41) Thomas Howard (39)
Thomas Anthony Howard (14) Eric George Hughes (42)
Alan Johnston (29) Christine Anne Jones (27) Gary
Philip Jones (18) Richard Jones (25) Nicholas Peter
Joynes (27) Anthony Peter Kelly (29) Michael David

Kelly (38) Carl David Lewis (18) David William Mather (19) Brian Christopher Mathews (38) Francis Joseph McAllister (27) John McBrien (18) Marion Hazel McCabe (21) Joseph Daniel McCarthy (21) Peter McDonnell (21) Alan McGlone (28) Keith McGrath (17) Paul Brian Murray (14) Lee Nicol (14) Stephen Francis O'Neill (17) Jonathon Owens (18) William Roy Pemberton (23) Carl William Rimmer (21) David George Rimmer (38) Graham John Roberts (24) Steven Joseph Robinson (17) Henry Charles Rogers (17) Colin Andrew Hugh William Sefton (23) Inger Shah (38) Paula Ann Smith (26) Adam Edward Spearritt (14) Philip John Steele (15) David Leonard Thomas (23) Patrik John Thompson (35) Peter Reuben Thompson (30) Stuart Paul William Thompson (17) Peter Francis Tootle (21) Christopher James Traynor (26) Martin Kevin Traynor (16) Kevin Tyrrell (15) Colin Wafer (19) Ian David Whelan (19) Martin Kenneth Wild (29) Kevin Daniel Williams (15) Graham John Wright (17)

Dante Alighieri was exiled from his city of Florence so he wrote *The Divine Comedy*. You could say that and it might be true enough. He could also add stuff up: all those cantos, not to mention the beats, stresses, syllables. Bea slips me Dante like my father did LSD when he smelled marijuana on me. I was thirteen. "Really, you can do better than that, can't you?" Mother said it was reverse psychology, but it really wasn't. At least my girlfriend *could* concentrate on the good stuff in the *Inferno* but, instead, she has set her eye on salvation and insists I read *Purgatorio*. Not the paradise either but purgatory. I say, "You are crazy." She says if you exchange 'ft' for 'z', it'd be crafty. *Foreigners*. She explains that Dante's purgatory is an island mountain you climb to heaven. To spite her, I read about the descending circles of hell when I'm waiting to deliver yet another meal, at *Speedy Delivery,* where I work part-time.

The Stadium is imposing. It opens up like a peach and never rots in its protective cage. It's a concrete pit of absolute symmetry or a squatting bug that rises up and falls in one grand gesture. We always feel justified, if naked, in its looming presence. My girlfriend hands me a flyer as we stand lost in our own thoughts. Someone gave her this at work. It pictures broken shackles or handcuffs and below it reads:

JESUS Can Set You Free!
YOUR SPECIAL INVITATION to an URGENT GOSPEL GATHERING
According to Bible prophecy, we are living in the last days. The signs of the end-time were clearly described many years ago by Bible prophets and apostles. Some of these signs were an increase of EARTHQUAKES, HEART ATTACKS due to stress, an escalation of STRANGE DISEASES, the major BREAKDOWN of the HOME, WARS, FAMINE and the deterioration of MORALS world wide. The Bible gives a great hope of the SECOND COMING of JESUS, who will return to rapture those who are born again, to ever be with HIM. JESUS IS COMING SOON! YOU MUST BE SAVED THE BIBLE WAY!
Bring the whole family, every night!
Special Speaker: Evangelist Johnny Carroll from Tennessee, U.S.A.
Service Schedule: Nightly at 7.30 (Except Monday & Tuesday) 10.00 AM Sunday
Date: January 3rd to January 21st
Place: First United Pentecostal Church
13054 -112 Street
Edmonton, Alberta
"Prayer Changes Things"

"But that was two months ago. We've missed out."

"Sorry," she says just like that.

"It's all your fault; because of you, I'll never be saved."

"If it was only that easy." She shivers in her coat.

"What if it was?!" I don't want to suffer for salvation. I want my kind of paradise now. Something like we've experienced this summer at our stadium. Something spectacular, soccer matches filled with a 40,000 crowd. Even at these numbers, our stadium seemed a half empty monster, an inferno. We stood on our plastic seats screaming *die you faker, die*! in the Women's U-19 semifinal between Canada and Brazil. *That wasn't offside! You call that a pass? Are you fucking blind?* Our throats had grown hoarse during the penalty shoot out; our screams lost like ice cream wrappers in a theatre of war. And Canada won. After the game, on our way to and in the subway station, among screams, foot stomping, chants and laughter, the crowd broke out into a spontaneous *O Canada*. We sang along, arms around each other. "One day, we'll have our own football songs," Bea said.

But then we had to climb high into the stands for the final between Canada and USA. We could see the world from up there yet everything got colder and thinner and lonelier. I'll take the concrete terraces in British football stadiums any day. It's my dream, to stand there. Just as I dream of death on the pitch, pressed into the pitch, suffocation. I dream of it at night. The sinews of an Adidas ball whisper Highbury and death on the green and I wake up with an erection. I know the names of the stadiums my favourite teams play: Highbury (I worship Arsenal), Anfield Road (*You'll Never Walk Alone* is my girlfriend's song), Elland Road, Stamford Bridge...yet I have never stepped foot on British soil. I think being British is being suffocated, with the inherited right to suffocate others.

"Pride, envy, anger, sloth, avarice, gluttony, lust. Nothing interesting to repent for," my girl says. We look at each other like enormous failures, undivine comedies and spectacular misses.

31

When Canada lost in the final, we didn't leave the stadium for an hour. We didn't want to be on the subway trains with more than 20,000 other frustrated, disappointed people. It was hard enough not to murder one another.

Encircling the giant arena, we walk down Stadium Road. It's grey, especially in winter, with businesses on one side and the Stadium and a large park on the other. Concrete fencing blocks access to the railroad tracks for blocks on end. We never meet anyone walking this road, and feel conspicuous, criminal just stepping over the cleared empty driveways and the less frequently shovelled sidewalks. We don't make eye contact with the drivers of straying, oncoming cars. The camera lens scrutiny unsettles us. Soon we will get into the tiny, scummy couple of blocks on 107A Avenue. The rundown claustrophobic funk will settle and melt like fresh snow, all before we reach 95th Street.

I pull Bea's toque off and mess up "the hair." She kicks my right ankle with her foot. When I bend over to smooth the bruise, and shake off the snow, she knees me in the bum. I stagger forward.

"Red card, you thug. I'm going to kill you." I run after her.

The Warning Bells: Heysel
The Globe and Mail
30 May, 1985
Brussels—At least 40 people were killed and more than 350 injured in a riot before the start of the European Cup final soccer game between Liverpool of England and Juventus of Italy at Heysel Stadium last night....

The trouble began because a section of the stadium was being shared by supporters of both clubs. Liverpool fans, thousands of whom had spent the day drinking in the city before attending the game attacked Italian supporters. They were joined by more English hooligans who broke down a protective barrier to join the fighting.

The panic spread swiftly as spectators were driven into a wedge at the southwest corner of the stadium. There they were faced with the horrifying choice of a 30-foot leap over a wall or escape onto the field.

Most of those able to do so took the latter choice and there was a loud crack audible around the grounds as the stone wall and wire fence surrounding the field were trampled down. Hundreds of people had spilled onto the field and it was not until they were dispersed that the extent of the damage became clear. Many bodies were trapped beneath the rubble of the wall and those able to drag themselves clear had made for the field. The scene of the disaster resembled the aftermath of an air raid, with clothing and discarded shoes heaped on the terraces.

I bang on the metal newspaper box at the bus stop, jammed. Then I turn away from its headlines. "You okay?"

Bea's throwing up, thankfully downwind from me. I can't handle vomit, my gagging reflex is beyond extraordinary.

She wipes her mouth. "Do you have a handkerchief?"

I hand her a Kleenex.

"Are you all right?"

She nods.

When I keep staring at her, she says, "It's your father. Makes me sick. The food didn't go down properly. He scares the hell out of me."

"Well I think I have more right to be frightened."

"Why is that?" she asks annoyed.

"You're only scared that people like my father exist. I have to live with the daily fear that I might turn into my father!"

Bea nods. Then she says, "Perhaps there are worse things to be."

"Such as?"

"*Scum of the earth,* an Irish/Polish boy I knew." She points to the newspaper box I've just been abusing. "He kicked one of those in because it swallowed two of his quarters."

33

Just the way she says scum of the earth, its wet softness, I can tell she's more than fucked this motherfucker. I look at the box with a strange jealousy and then turn angrily to look at her. Thankfully, she grabs her stomach and turns from me. And I have to take a few steps forward and cover my ears or we'll both be retching.

Soon after, we get on the 5 bus. It's a short strip but I keenly watch the tattoo parlors, Salvation Army stores, holed up groceries, electronic stores, bridal shops all interspersed with churches. It's true God really loves the suffering and the poor. We get off on 118 Ave. by the used bookstore, the *Wee-Book Inn*. My girl searches the spoils for classics and books about buildings, mainly churches. I play with the resident tabby. The grimy, troll of a man at the counter snorts at Bea. I think she must have told him once, before I met her, where she's from. Even so, every time she comes in, he leans forward and asks, "Where are you from?"

I don't get it. It's like a joke between them, two foreigners, except they're speaking English.

"Guess," she says. "I lie by the River Troja, once I was owned by an order of bishops, I became a city in 1321. Round and round I've come, I've been Czech, I've been Prussian, I've been Polish. I'm known for my beautiful tapestries, rich fabric trade from sixteenth century on, and the baroque church off the town square. I've been burned down by Russian hands more than once." She winks at the man at the counter because he told her his mother was Russian although he's Czech. And then Bea grows serious. "A work camp for prisoners of war lay once at my head...my cemetery is enormous but my 6,600 residents are fleeing me by train for large cities. What city am I?"

"That could be anywhere in Eastern Europe," the man says.

"Everywhere," my girlfriend adds flippantly and pulls at the sleeve of my coat. We leave.

10 Concentric Circles or Relevant Facts regarding FA Cup Semi Final Match between Liverpool and Nottingham Forest on April 15, 1989:

10. The build up of fans around the Leppings Lane area increased dramatically when many coaches arrived around 2 PM after experiencing delays from road works and police searches along the way.

9. Because Liverpool fans had been allocated the Leppings Lane end of the ground—the smaller end, from 2.30 PM 10,000 people with tickets for the Leppings Lane end tried to enter three gates, and seven turnstiles. People with tickets for the West Stand (located above the terracing) also had to enter by the same three gates.

8. As the volume of those trying to enter at the Leppings lane end increased by the minute, an officer requested that the kick-off be delayed in order to reassure the crowd that there was no urgency. The request was denied.

7. Marshall radioed Chief Superintendent Duckenfield and requested that the exit gates be opened. Duckenfield ordered to open gate C at 2.52 PM and police directed football supporters through the gate.

6. The people headed toward the most obvious entrance to the terraces which was through the tunnel opposite into pens 3 and 4. In previous years police and/or stewards would stand at the entrance to the tunnel if these central pens had reached capacity and would direct fans to the side pens. In 1989, however, no such direction took place as people headed into the already overcrowded pens.

5. Inside the pens people were dead and dying. Faces were crushed up against the two-metre perimeter fencing; people were vomiting and turning blue in the face. Supporters were packed so tightly that many were dead standing up. Many still conscious were trying to break down the sharptooth, and bent back at 45 degrees, fencing with their hands.

4. Those who had managed to climb over the fencing or

escape when a perimeter gate was briefly opened also struggled to free their fellow fans.

3. Many police officers began to assist in trying to get people out. Unaware, other officers pushed fans back inside the pens from which they had momentarily escaped when the perimeter gate opened.

2. Six minutes after 3 PM the referee halted the game.

1. Bodies were laid out on the pitch and the injured wandered around dazed and confused. Fans tore down advertising boards to act as stretchers and ferried fans to the far end of the pitch in the hope that they would receive treatment.

I hate grocery stores. They're underworlds: negotiating, peeling off sleepwalkers, prophets, crazies, welfare cases, like an artichoke. Trash begets trash. But this Safeway on the corner of 82 Street and 118 Avenue is all right, at least you avoid the enlightened, trendy-thriftiness that comes with student poverty south of Whyte Avenue.

"I'm going to take out money, okay?" I say to my girl as we leave the store with minimal essentials.

Bea nods and heads out the door with the bags.

"Why don't you support our strike by buying your food somewhere else?" I hear a man say and turn to see him approach Bea right at the door. She walks past him. I shake my head as I enter my PIN quickly.

When I look up again, I see the man has stepped in front of her, blocking her way. "I asked you a question. At least you could answer me."

I press *chequing,* annoyed with the slow cash-machine.

I hear her say, "I don't have a car. I make less than some of you who are striking. I don't think I need to answer any of your questions."

I quickly grab my card and take my money. I hear a female voice saying, "But don't you get it? That's the point. That's precisely why you should support us...."

"Leave her alone." I push myself between Bea and the four people that have surrounded her. They are all dressed in heavy coats and placards. I take her bags out of her hands. "Go harass someone else, asshole," I say to the man who's been blocking Bea's way. I get right up close so my nose is nearly touching his and the cardboard hanging from a string around his neck digs awkwardly into my knee.

He sneers at me and even though he could probably level me in a second I'm tempted to shove him. But I just stare at him and he walks away.

When we're out of their hearing range I say, "Why didn't you tell them that you wanted to go somewhere else? Why didn't you just tell them that I was too lazy to go to *Save on Foods* so we came here...."

She shrugs and doesn't answer.

"Why are you always looking for trouble?"

"It's none of their fucking business."

Before you can enter the fightvids.co.uk web site you need to agree to these terms. If you are affiliated with any government, anti-Piracy group, or any other related group, or were formally a worker of one, you can NOT enter or use this web site: you cannot access any of its files and you cannot view any of the HTML files. All the objects on this site are PRIVATE property. DO NOT ENTER—otherwise you'll be violating code 431.322.12 of the Internet Privacy Act signed by Bill Clinton in 1995. You can NOT threaten my ISP or any person(s) or company storing these files, cannot prosecute any person(s) affiliated with this page which includes family, friends or individuals who run or enter this web site.

Purchase Fightvids Video 1—approximately 3 hours of Hooligan Footage including: Euro96 England v Scotland, Bristol City v Rovers, Italy v England, Cardiff v Swansea, Stoke v Birmingham, Portsmouth v Sheff Utd,

Ireland v England (1995), Juventus v Liverpool (Heysel)
All content sold in these videos are clippings from press and news reports.
THIS IS FOOTBALL FIGHT CLUB and there is only ONE rule in fight club.
Please feel free to leave any comments on fight club here

PUSSYS
Posted on Mar 9, 2004, 9.34 AM
by WOTTHEFUCKULOOKINAT (no login)
ALL U FOOTBALL HOOLIGANS ARE FAGGOTS IF YOU WANT A PROPER SCRAP GET DOWN BRISTOL CITY CENTRE ON THE 13TH MARCH IVE GOTTA FIRM WAITING TO TEACH YOU LITTLE GIRLS A LESSON..HA

cunt
Posted on Apr 2, 2004, 9.35 AM
by sam jolly (no login)
you chat shit come down southampton and i ll make sure i cut your fucking bollocks off with a steak knive you little wanker fuck all your greasey fat mums. you fucking pussy!!!!!!!!!!

The darkness has tucked our imperfections in like a woolly scarf. We have abandoned the bus for the solid footing of the street swollen with snow. I start rubbing my ears and stare into the windows of the houses we pass. My girlfriend hands me back my toque and I take it gratefully. "The hair," "violent and disaffected," has resigned itself to the night, and only the awkwardness of such a manoeuvre prevents me from kissing the top of my girlfriend's head. Bea's still sullen and confounded. I step into Bea to feel her; put my arm around her waist. But she elbows me and I'm about to pull away when I realize she wants me to look to the right.

Out of one of the bungalows a man runs out in a hastily

thrown on parka, unzipped boots and a scarf that hangs at his side. He slams the door so hard it bounces off the door frame and remains open. In the dark it's hard to tell his age, but he speaks to himself in Chinese. A minute later, a woman appears at the door, wearing a thin, black, flowered bathrobe. She leaves the door open. The illusion of fragility as she hurries after the man. Her dark hair spills down from the top of her head. She grabs his arm and he pulls back. Their voices rise into the night and you can tell, you can, what they are saying. The man pushes her away. But the woman pulls at the man and steps backwards toward the door. Stubbornly slow at first but finally yielding, the man lets himself be pulled back across the empty street, up the driveway, back up the stairs into his home. A transfer of weight back and forth, control, balance, give and acceleration. Like a dummy swerve or Beardsley shimmy.

And we watch this shamelessly, caught up. In the dark we stand a little longer and then walk on silently.

"But there was a reason why they put up that blue fence and protective barriers at Hillsborough. Those cops must all have seen pictures of Heysel. Must have thought it was just another out of control football mob going off, out to destroy each other and everything else in their path."

"But it wasn't. It was us...."

Bea seriously considers this and then asks, "How many people died in Hillsborough?"

"95. And a boy, who had been in a coma, died later." I can't shut myself up. "Of those who died, 89 were men, seven women. The majority was under 30 and more than a third under twenty. The youngest to die was a ten-year-old boy."

She doesn't say anything. She keeps a part of herself to herself.

With an expansive and loud stretch, I grab her to me, crushing her. "The cause of death was crush asphyxia." She puts her head into my chest. "Most deaths occurred in pen

39

3, the remainder in pen 4. Most people died at the front of the pens," I whisper.

"I want to get my toque back," she says biting down on the plastic tip of my hood string, pulls and releases it.

"All right," I tell her but don't let go. We stand together, our bagged fruit bruised, entangled, sulking between us.

And we dream: the green, the green, the green. The sun is shining on Hillsborough stadium. In the Leppings Lane turnstile, there's a body after body. It's a Liverpool away game, your girlfriend's favourite team, in an FA Cup semifinal against Nottingham Forest. She's got a crush on this L'Pool player named Peter Beardsley, but with her luck you bet he's not even going to be warming the bench today. She's antsy. Even though you've left three hours before, there was road construction and now you've got only half an hour to get in before the kickoff. And there are so, so many people. She winces, you grab her hand, she smiles but you can see it's like she's burned herself and can't stay still. She wants to strangle the cop that insists on searching her. She says "ridiculous" even though there are millions of more obscene things she could say, and people around you say them. As you continue on, you point to the sides: *we can get in that way*. But she wants to follow the people into the tunnel and you're being pushed along. She wants to be at the centre, where all the best shit happens. She wants to scream, "You kick like a girl, arsehole," and not be ashamed because there are other people yelling with her. You wouldn't mind sitting up above in the West stand. But, according to your girl it's on the terraces that god kisses the football fan. And the terraces are cheaper than a seat.

It's overcrowded once you both get out of the tunnel, barely any room. Pens 5 and 6 are not full at all and you smirk *because you told her so* and you could've had plenty of space if she only listened to you. But this doesn't last long. You have to push through, "fuck you, fuck you, my girlfriend's pregnant arseshitkisser," you yell, lie and even though it's rough going you elbow your way toward the middle of pen 4. "Stupid people. Stupid cops, they've probably just closed off the tunnel and lots of people will be irked because they'll miss kickoff," you say to your girlfriend. But she's all concentrating. She needs to make an effort to hold onto her program and ignores you. It's still ten minutes to kickoff and it's already overcrowded. You stare back at where you came from and you don't think they've closed the tunnel because there's more people pushing on and they're pushing this way. You hate crowds. Hate crowds more than people on their own. And why do people have to push so hard, football won't fucking save ya, won't blow you off. Somebody's elbow is digging deep into your back and somebody else's knee is just below the cheek of your ass. You realize you're packed so tight you can't turn your head to see and tell the bastards off. Your girlfriend gets swept, pushed forward violently. It's too packed for her to move too far but you can't move your head to see so it's as if she has disappeared, forever. You yell "fuck, come on that's my g...nd" but the air inside of you is pushed up and out and you start fighting to stay breathing and not get trampled. Your feet are no longer on the ground. Something's wrong. The whistle and the game starts and you try yelling her name but it comes out only as foreign, guttural sound. The last thing you hear before you reach the bottom of hell is the sound of a ball, synthetic leather, expertly struck and climbing, into a faint....

Ten Questions You Must Ask Yourself
in Warsaw

WHERE DO YOU START KNOWING A CITY? (30 JULY, 2001)
Below, Wisla coils and coos in the cool breeze, the dark sus-
pension of disbelief. Cars speed along the Wislostrada. The
lights of Praga, across the river, beseech in the night.
Teenagers sit on Wybrzeze Gdanskie with their beer and
vodka. Some laugh but most are quiet. Thoughts grow
scales, like dragons. One church slips into the habit of the
other. When Baska turns from the river, she walks into the
shadow of the church dedicated to the visitation of the
Virgin. She stares up the freestanding fifteenth century bel-
fry. A lightning rod. She turns left. From the New Town, she
heads toward the Old Town's Square.

Down on Freta St. a band plays an acoustic set of classical, rag-tag jazz: street music.

She sits on the curb to listen. The cobbled street and four-
storeys-tall, pastel-coloured buildings, hip-to-hip, create a
natural amphitheatre. A young man sits down beside her.
She's almost sure he has followed her from the river. Finally
he scoots over to her and she smiles at the smoothness and
awkwardness of the movement.

"Marek."

"Baska." She takes his hand; it's not much bigger than
hers. He's been to New York he tells her, worked there for a
while. Didn't like North America much. His hair is dirty
blond, cut short. He seems so sure of himself, it's annoying
yet oddly reassuring. She looks back at the band.

"You like the music?"

She nods. "It has its charm, like this entire city."

He taps her camera briefly with his right knuckle.
"Taking pictures of the seventeenth-century buildings? You
know that's a bunch of bullshit. After the Uprising, the

Germans razed the city to the ground."

"I know."

"What's worse is that cities, like Szczecin, got coerced, forced to demolish buildings that survived the war just so the same materials could be used to rebuilt Warsaw's pre-war buildings."

His sarcasm doesn't taint her.

"Your Polish isn't bad," he says finally.

"I was born in Poland; I lived here until I was eleven years old."

"In Warsaw?"

"No." She waits. "In a little Silesian town."

He senses her irritation, sidesteps it. "Look what I found." He hands her an early chestnut in its green sheath.

Baska takes it shyly and attempts to pull off its skin, but it's too hard.

"When ripe, the green sides open and widen faithfully," he says as she stares at him. "Inside the nut is brown, and lustrous as a horse's coat. Do you have a pen?" he asks.

"Yes." And as she's taking out the pen, she realizes what it's for. She'd rather he not but she doesn't stop him as he jabs the point through the skin down to the white pulp. He pulls out the nut; hides it in the palm of her hand. The music ends, fervent sound gone. The musicians, in pairs or threes, disappear down the cobbled street.

"I have some friends who play in a band; you should come and see them."

"What do they play?"

"Some of their own stuff." Then as if deciding on something he adds, "Well, mostly they cover old punk, like The Clash."

"Everywhere I go it's techno, DJs and hip hop. I'd love to hear some punk. But I should probably get moving, the hostel at Smolna St., where I'm staying, is at least half-an-hour's walk from here." Baska rolls her eyes. "They have an 11 PM curfew."

43

He smiles. "My friend's band is playing tomorrow at Szara Strefa on Marszalkowska not far from the Palace of Culture and Science; it's not Stodola or Ground Zero but the show starts at nine.... I could meet you right here earlier. Four or five? We could go together."

"Five's super."

WHAT ARE YOU DOING IN WARSAW? (GIOVANNI BATTISTA MONTINI: 30 JULY, 1923) In the solid, dead heat, the curtains grow limp. Battista puts down his prayer book. The last of the July heat sits on his shoulders. He hears the tram-brakes from Ujazdowskie Street, their hyena screech chafes like his stiff white collar. And the chirping Poles outside, restless and cocky even in the heat, their whistling and their endless declensions. He tries but he just doesn't have an ear, the edge for the damned language. The futility of his position immobilizes him; a supposed Vatican diplomat, he can't communicate outside of the chapel and the unattended Latin Mass. The Nunciature on Ksiazeca has become an Italian refuge in the middle of Warsaw. With the Italian newspapers, food and meal times, Nuncio Lauri, Vatican's Italian Representative, has sufficiently blocked out the squabbles and slights of the arrogant Polish bishops. And now Lauri has left for a vacation in Czechoslovakia. Battista thinks back to his school for the Vatican's diplomats at the Gregorian University in Rome. He bitterly agrees that learning moral theology with father Arregui, discussing the distance from which one might properly view copulating animals, is applicable to his diplomatic duties in Warsaw: watching flies mate is the most excitement he's had in weeks.

As he exits the Nunciature, he looks toward St. Alexander's church. His gaze travels along two towers guarding the neo-classical columned entrance and behind it the Roman-Pantheon-inspired dome. Some of the passersby nod to him on account of his priestly tunic. Others ignore him. After he crosses Aleje Jerozolimskie he turns right into the first quiet street off of Nowy Swiat. He avoids the traffic by swerving a block off the main street, onto Galczynskiego St. Walking, he hears distinctive notes, purposefully heavy-handed, like someone taking pleasure in running up stone steps in high-heeled boots. The piano player reaches a high note and comes back to a soft pa-da, tam-da, a nocturne. He gave up piano practice three years ago but cannot resist being drawn into the music. He nears the window. The music stops. While he listens for it to begin again, the second-storey window's paper-yellow curtains sway and he sees a young woman behind them. He hears a soft, "Nie odchodz," but doesn't understand, steps back blushing and continues on his way.

At the statue of Copernicus, Battista sits down. He's waiting for Carlo Chiarlo, his supervisor at the Nuciature now that Nucio Lauri is vacationing. The Tuscan sometimes attends the evening mass at the Holy Cross Church. After the parishioners leave, he spots Chiarlo. Battista crosses Krakowskie Przedmiescie and calls after the man. "Father Chiarlo, Father Chiarlo attesa, per piacere!"

The man turns and grins. "Father Montini, good to see you about. I see you have changed your mind."

"About what?"

"About there being nothing to see in Warsaw." He winks. Battista ignores the playful grin on Chiarlo's face.

"Where are we walking, Father?"

"I need to see a man about a watch."

The Poles around them tower in height and girth, not only the men but also some of the women. Battista suspects where Chiarlo is leading him. He's heard that Chiarlo enjoys walking for hours on end in Warsaw's Jewish quarter. His superior hums an aria from Mozart's *Don Giovanni*. From Gesia they turn onto Lubiecka then Mila. Above the doorways, the twilight of the evening casts patchy shadows over the wooden signs on metal poles. The industry around Battista feels cosmopolitan yet eastern, rather comparable to

45

Venice than what he has experienced in Rome. Names and signs advertize services and merchandise. He catches bits of foreign words "Lecz..." "...zny." A boy, in a yarmulke and earlocks, chased by another, runs dead smack into Chiarlo's stomach. Chiarlo places his hands on the boy's shoulders, "Rallentare, ragazzo," he says and with a shake of the head turns the boy neatly around and sends him on his way. Battista follows Chiarlo into the clockmaker's.

"Father Chiarlo, your father's watch is as good as new. In fact, if I was not the tactful man I am, I would suggest it's working better than ever before." The Jew is an attractive, tall man with black glasses and a greying beard. Fedora hat covers his head and hides his earlocks. Battista cannot help but notice his slender hands. They had nodded to each other when Battista entered but now the man comes up to him. "...po francusku?" the man asks Chiarlo and turns to Battista. "Bienvenue, Père Montini. You'll be surprised how much you enlarge your circle of acquaintance in Warsaw if you use your French, Father. Can I help you with anything today?"

"I need an alarm clock," Battista responds in French, pleasantly surprised. "And that one, that one would suit me well I think...."

WHO ARE YOU IN WARSAW? (30 JULY, 2001) "Jestem studentka." Baska's arrived on a Polish passport. It is her second night at the hostel; she's unable to decide which language to speak. She has exchanged English hellos with the Swedish girls in her room, but mostly she's been quiet. An American girl enters their room and engages a Polish mother and daughter, travelling together, in a discussion.

The girl says, "I don't have pockets full of money. I took out a loan to travel around the world. Thought I should, before I go back to school to study political science and law, so I can change what is going on in my country. You cannot imagine what injustices take place under the guise of democracy; the violence and crime in our cities is just disgusting. Warsaw is peaceful and quiet." Baska's sympathy for the stranger is waning. "Living under the Communist regime all those years probably saved you from the capitalist corruption in America. Americans have no real right to protest, they can arrest you for no apparent reason...you are lucky you don't live in America."

The American notices Baska's frown and asks her where she's from. "Canada," she tells her.

"Then you must know what it's like."

"There are poor and homeless people in Canada but people do have the right to protest laws they don't agree with. I thought that was the case in United States...."

"No, not at all. Foreigners think so, but they are wrong."

Baska looks around, hoping the two Swedes, the Polish women and the girl from Ireland are taking all the American girl says with a healthy dose of skepticism.

In the washroom, Baska faces herself in the mirror; appreciating the silence. She is surprised by the talkative American who reclaims her flattened, threadbare toothbrush of the edge of the sink.

"Sometimes, I just have to tell them the truth, maybe it's not tactful, but I do...."

Baska half-smiles, nods and the American girl leaves her.

Before she goes to sleep, Baska sits down with a map of the city. She lightly circles her early morning finds: the Evangelical Church and *Zacheta* Modern Art Gallery. The church, round and domed, seemed to spin her right into the gallery: classical, columned and square. Her excitement at beauty and ugliness is tempered with bitterness; her Polish cousins cannot afford a week-long trip to Warsaw. And they certainly cannot afford the Polish books with which she's slowly filling her whole suitcase. She looks up from the map and, out of a small window near the ceiling, she sees a piece of it. Soviet-built and 231m high, the Palace of Culture and Science stands tall in testimony: to Stalin's generosity, to all things erect, sandstone, ambitious, even alien, to the peaceful and quiet life in Poland. Like a dead star at Warsaw's centre, the building dominates the city. But to be confronted with it in this quiet room, in a brief frame of the city skyline, is different. Intimate. Takes your breath away—a little, she thinks. She writes belated birthday wishes on the postcard of the monument to the Warsaw Uprising. Sometimes she's late but she never misses her mother's birthday.

WHAT WAS YOUR MOTHER LIKE IN WARSAW? (FROM THE UNOFFICIAL COURTSHIP OF TERESKA ROGOWSKA: WARSAW 1965) Tereska squeezes her dance partner's hand as they grin foolishly at each other and step into the Krakowiak, bowing. Their quick steps make crazy zigzags in the track's clay. Tereska is exhilarated to lose herself in the rhythm of a thousand dancers moving in step. It's the feeling of being full, at the edge of spilling; she gets it while dancing. She nearly cries out, faster. And as if obeying her, the mazur comes on next. The Polonaise is their finale and they bow before Party's first secretary, Wladyslaw Gomulka. They're at the 10th Anniversary Stadium to celebrate the end of harvest, their annual thanksgiving. By the end of the dance the rest of the stadium joins them: gymnasts and other athletes. And it's as if the stadium is bursting at its seams and she, her partner and another couple from their group dance themselves right into the middle of the crowd. Tereska feels beautiful in her costume; her wreath is tightly pinned in her hair, streaming ribbons. She is a daredevil in the red high-heeled boots. A man in shorts, T-shirt, running shoes and hair so blond it's almost white grabs her hand. His eyes are bright green. He's a wonderful dancer. She is separated from her friends but this only makes her more reckless and giddy. She trades partners once more before a boy in a goral costume leads her toward the dancing troops and she bumps into Heniek from her dance group.

Despite exhaustion, numb feet and legs, that night

48

Tereska lies in her bed for hours before she can fall asleep. This whole week in Warsaw has been the best time she's ever had. Every day after practising till 5 PM, they'd eat dinner and go to student coffee houses in the basements of Warsaw's Old Town. There, if they were lucky, they'd get to listen to the student cabaret. Even the songs were political, passionate and lively. In those places the cigarette smoke was so thick she could barely see her friends across the table.

Tereska does not want to go back to Kietrz. Even though Janek is there. She has watched him, his friends, since the first time they met. His friends talk a lot, drink hard. Janek is importunely quiet and serious. She's seen him laugh, shake his head but never join in; he looks bored by their drunken antics. He's biding his time. She likes his dark hair and how tall he is. All she knows is that his family came back from Canada; they were there a year or two and then came back. They own a car, a black American Pontiac. Last year he offered her and her three friends a ride back home from the cinema. Jaska and Jadzka lived in Kozlowka but she and her friend Wojtek were going to Rogozany. She and the girls sat in the back, while Wojtek, at the front, asked about the car. Jadzka leaned over and asked, "How do you say, you have a nice car, in English?" Janek seemed to think for a while and, looking into the rearview mirror at Tereska, he said *"You have beautiful eyes."* "Ooh," Jadzka exclaimed, "It must be so wonderful to know another language—beside Russian." When he stopped at her house, Tereska got out of the car and ran inside.

At first this older boy with a car was far from her mind as she finished her literature compositions. Or as she lined up on the dance floor in practice. "Tereska, straighten your back," her dance teacher frowned last week but she laughed, while led through a Polonaise. Her teacher praised her: "You make every partner that you dance with look good. That's a gift." Tereska is happy. She'll finish school next year and she gets to go out with her friends on the weekends and there is

49

a theatre group she'd like to join. But Warsaw is different, makes her think that perhaps she can be different. She remembers last week walking out from their final rehearsal before they left for Warsaw. She stopped on top of the stairs, and backed up into the doorway where he couldn't see her and she could watch him. Janek was standing across from the building, smoking, looking left and right. After he finished his cigarette, he left. Tereska waited another five minutes before she walked down the stairs toward her bus stop.

WHY DID YOU COME HERE? (31 JULY, 2001) Marek asks. Baska never answers a question if she can help it. When she first arrived in Canada, her classmates thought it inconceivable that she couldn't understand what they said. They thought she was willingly silent, stubbornly dumb and they resented it. Perhaps they were upset about the homework not knowing English got her out of. They found her suspect. She felt suspect. Long after she began to read, speak and think in English, Baska had nothing to say, to most. She tells Marek, "I prefer when clues accumulate and reverberate like churches, like a good punk song, like patriotic fervour. Is that suspect?"

"Not suspect, or romantic either," Marek finally says. "You're a typical Polish bullshitter, contrariness comes with it." They are sitting against the orange brick of the Barbican. Baska could pretend offence, but she's not offended.

"Why did you really come here?" he asks.

"Back in Edmonton I found a book called *The Documents in Communist Affairs 1977* and in it was a speech by Pope Paul VI during Edward Gierek's visit to the Vatican."

"And?" He frowns.

"Pope Paul said..." She stands above Marek, changing from Polish to English. "Excellency, Poland is very dear to us because of the personal memories which link us to her. An all-destroying fury of war has rolled over Warsaw, extinguishing countless human lives and leaving utter destruction in its wake. However, the will of the Polish people, then motivated them, as a matter of honour, to do everything to make this city, the symbol of the people's oneness and its desire to live, rise from the ashes once again...."

"This isn't our Pope?"

"An Italian. His name was Giovanni Battista Enrico Antonio Maria Montini. He came to Warsaw in 1923 for four months of diplomatic service."

"And I should care because...."

"Because Gianco Zincone said, 'Montini's mind, that of the intellectual, was full of doubts and fine distinctions' and this didn't make him a popular pope."

"Intellectuals? Could use less of those."

"He liked to watch championship soccer matches on TV."

"I hate soccer and the fuckers who watch it," Marek says flicking dried blades of grass.

"Well then you'll definitely burn in hell."

"I'm kidding you." He nudges her.

"When Paul VI sat in front of his TV and saw man landing on the moon, he saw God."

"Hmm."

"And did you know he kept his Polish alarm clock which he bought in Warsaw in 1923 right until his death in 1977. And the day he died it rang at 9.40 PM (time of his death) instead of its usual time of 6 AM...."

"I have met all kinds of tourists but you're...."

"I'm not a tourist...and you asked."

The first long awkward silence settles on them. There's something about Marek that Baska's aware of but today in this sun refuses to accept.

"You recognize that?" Marek asks.

Baska listens closer, a familiar melody and voice. She nods.

"Let's go." He grabs her hand and together they half-run

toward the King's Palace.

There a sizable crowd is beginning to gather. On a great stage set up in the square, Baska recognizes Krzysztof Krawczyk. Krawczyk, the Polish Elvis, her dad's favourite singer, now middle aged and pot bellied, is singing his heart out. She and Marek grin at each other. It's a typically cheesy love song. Marek puts his arm around her neck and faking drunken ecstasy he sings along with Krawczyk.

After a minute of this, a man behind them tells Marek to shut up.

Marek turns around, "What did you say?"

"I said shut up. Some people are trying to enjoy the music."

"But I am enjoying the music...." Marek turns back and keeps singing.

The man puts his hand on Marek shoulder and Marek turns around and brushing off his arm he says nonchalantly. "I would prefer if you didn't touch me."

"Marek, please." Baska intervenes.

Marek puts his arm back around her and speaks up. "This girl came all the way from Canada to see Krzysztof Krawczyk!" He shakes his finger in front of the man's nose. Then he points it at Baska. "She loves Krzysztof Krawczyk! She lives Krzysztof Krawczyk! Come on," he said, "Show them your Krawczyk tattoo." Marek starts pulling up Baska's T-shirt. "It's on her left breast." She slaps his hands, pulls, and backs away from him. "Basiu, Basiu," Marek wails, "wroc, no co, teraz nigdy mi nie uwierza." Baska keeps walking away.

Marek finally gives up and walks toward her among dirty looks and insults from the people around them.

When they sit down under the Sigmund's column, Marek adds, "I was just defending my fundamental right."

"To be an asshole?" she asks.

"Maybe I'm mistaken but it's still my right."

"Sure is."

"Let's have a beer before we head to Szara Strefa." He gets up expecting her to follow. When she doesn't, he turns around and shakes his head. Gestures elaborately with his arms, "Come on tourist, the tour's not over."

WHY DID YOU COME HERE? (ITALIAN DIVERSION 2, THE VATICAN: NOVEMBER, 1977) Paul VI, Giovanni Battista Montini is 80 years old. And he is tired. A man of "infinite courtesy," that's what they say about him, he turns for the priest helping him into his vestments. Today he is meeting Edward Gierek, the First Secretary of Poland. In Warsaw at 26, Montini was someone altogether different, a boy really. After his arrival in Warsaw, he sent his parents a postcard of the Russian Orthodox Cathedral, which Poles destroyed within the first few weeks of his stay. He watched them gleefully pulling the Cathedral down, he hated them for their smallness; he didn't understand the context. Why would Poles destroy something so beautiful just because it was Russian? But history repeats its lessons until we're too tired to learn....

"His Excellency Edward Gierek is waiting, Your Holiness."

"Yes, yes," Battista says gently, "We must not keep him waiting."

Gierek is a solid, good-looking man at 64. Well dressed, he appears sure of himself. Battista is dwarfed by the man; he only weighs 154 pounds.

"Your Holiness." Gierek begins, "I wish to convey to you, Your Holiness, expressions of deep respect and best wishes of the Polish nation and of the supreme authorities of the Polish People's Republic." Gierek's voice is loud and thundering, quite appropriate for public speeches but rather obnoxious in a private audience.

Battista nods and settles in his chair, the arthritis in his hip keeps bothering him.

Gierek sits down and begins his speech, "Universally

appreciated is the consistence with which Your Holiness spares no effort to read correctly the signs of our times." He gestures widely with his arm. Licks his thin lips. Grows typically red horns.

Giovanni Battista keeps a smile on his face as he listens. Behind Gierek a man is standing stiffly beside a sheet covered object. Ah, the sculpture, he remembers.

"European nations are waiting for a slow-down of the armaments race, for effective prevention of the spread of nuclear weapons, for a ban on the production of new instruments of destruction and a liquidation of existing arsenals." The Pole pauses and his tail unfurrows. The tail beats against the reception-room's floor tiles in time with the man's words. He continues to read from his notes. "It is precisely because of this that my country fully supports the new Soviet proposals on these weighty questions."

The blond devil's tongue nearly hangs to the floor. Even so, Battista doesn't envy Gierek's position. Having to court the Soviet Union while trying to sedate his disgruntled, unhappy people. But Gierek's own pockets hang heavy with loot. And now his foreign loans, which at first brought a false prosperity in Poland, are bringing the country to ruin. Cardinal Wyszynski has not been silent.

"At the time of their liberation struggles, Poles wrote on their banners the lofty call "For your freedom and ours." Through the gallantry of its soldiers and resistance fighters combating the Nazi aggression...."

Battista leans back. If all else fails, blame it on the Nazis. He wouldn't put it past Gierek to know of his anti-Fascist sympathies, and for trying to play them.

"The price of that freedom was the annihilation of more than six million Polish men and women, among them many thousands of Catholic clergymen martyred by the occupant." Battista imagines himself a different man, grabbing Gierek by lapels, spinning him in circles to shake the evil and greed out of him.

"Mindful of the lessons of history, Poland has chosen the socialist social system and a tested orientation in foreign policy, it has chosen alliances which offer reliable guarantees of security and development."

It seems to Giovanni Battista that choice had little to do with it. In his mind's eye, he puts Gierek back down. Gierek's tail and horns disappear. Men are made, Battista thinks, knows. Just as he was when he was asked, "Acceptasne electionem de te canonice factam in Summum Pontifice?" (Do you accept your election as Supreme Pontiff according to the Canons?) Try saying no.

"We were building on ashes, amidst ruins and graves. We have attained much. We have raised our towns and villages from rubble, expanded industry, developed science and culture. Every Pole is sure of a job today, and whole youth has possibilities of education."

Giovanni nods to himself, wishes that all what Gierek says was true.

"Your Holiness' kind disposition toward Poland, our nation, is known in our country. We reciprocate it, expressing the conviction that this sympathy will ever accompany the Poles, that the moral authority of Your Holiness and the policy of the Holy See will continue to support the cause of peace and cooperation between nations." Finally the real reason for Gierek's visit. He's asking for Battista's blessing. Gierek stops speaking and turns to his delegation. The man that had been standing behind Gierek pulls off the sheet that was draping the sculpture.

"Your Holiness? May I ask you to accept this? The artist has named it "The Auschwitz Gehenna." It epitomizes much of the Polish nation's past and largely symbolizes our respect for the person to whom we present this gift."

Giovanni Battista rises and lightly embraces Gierek. Gierek is surprised but willing to milk this opportunity for all the good press he can.

"God sees all, my friend," Battista tells him. And then

adds into the man's ear, "Your time, like mine, is running out." He pats the man on the back and faces the sculpture. He imagines this is what purgatory might look like, and the careful, humble man he is, he's thankful to God for a sneak preview....

DO YOU BELONG IN WARSAW? (31 JULY, 2001) "It's a game." Marek speaks English to her. Baska plays along, pretending she doesn't speak Polish. He leans over, puts his arm around her shoulder. "She is my girlfriend. She thinks I am hot stuff," he says in English, making smooching sounds; he kisses her neck. She laughs but doesn't push him away. She shakes hands with the shaggy haired Andrzej. His black T-shirt says DIE PIGS. She points to it. "Cool."

"Tank you," he says. Scratches his head.

"He is drummer," Marek says. In order not to laugh, she doesn't look at him.

"This guy is a shit." He taps the tall, red haired boy on the shoulder. *The shit,* she thinks he means, turns out to be the lead singer, Pawel. Something in the way Pawel looks at her takes her aback.

"Marek," she finally says, becoming embarrassed the joke has gone on this far.

"Did you hear that?" he yells in Polish and hugs her so she's facing away from his friends. "I've taught her how to say my name in Polish. Isn't she cute?"

"Um. Marek, we need to get up there," Pawel says.

"Spoko. Yeah, have a good show." He hugs Pawel and slaps him on the back. She nods to the other two guys before they walk away.

Marek pulls her with him to the bar where he orders two beers and pays with the money she hands to him. She wants to talk to him, tell him the joke is stupid. But the music starts and *kapital* begin tyrannizing their guitar strings. Then the drums kick in. Everything gets better with the lead singer. He ignores everything but the microphone.

They do a surprisingly good version of "Guns of Brixton" and "The Call Up." Then there is a song in Polish Pawel introduces as his own. The song after that reverts back to English and the melody is unfamiliar but the words are not. *You ask me again, can't tell which letter this is. To write you back as soon as I can. How far I've gotten today? In the art of flying, the most difficult of arts. Every morning I take the elevator near to the roof. In our neighbourhood this building is the tallest of all. Everyday I look from it at the world. What will happen when I finally take that step?*

"Marek, the music is different but that's Lady Pank, Lady Pank lyrics translated into English. That's wicked."

"Shh." He pulls her up from the table by the stage and closer to the bathroom door.

...Generally speaking, life is brutal; besides that, everything's wonderful.

"Are you a fan?"

"*A fan?* Shut up," he hisses.

"Why?" She's hurt but clueless. "They're singing Lady Pank in English, I think that's cool."

"Shut up. They don't know they are playing Lady Pank."

"Pawel doesn't know he's singing a Lady Pank song?"

"Pawel knows. We translated it together. The rest of the guys don't."

"Why not?" She shakes her head. "Lady Pank had good songs—not like these new Polish bands I've heard."

"Lady Pank is eighties. Anyway, everybody thinks all Polish music *jest pojebana*. Do you think Polish people want to listen to Polish music?"

"I don't understand."

"Don't understand. Don't understand. What are you? Stupid? Do you listen to Polish music in Edmonston?"

"It's Edmonton...sometimes...that's not the point...."

"Wierze ci jak kurwa cholerze...."

"Fuck you." She uses English.

"Fucks you, fucks you." He sounds threatening, stupid

and cruel at the same time.

She turns away from him and bumps straight into Pawel. She had not realized the band had stopped playing and they were behind them. Marek grabs her arm from behind. "Leave me alone," she says in English.

"Mow po polsku," Marek says and turns her around roughly. "We're all Polish here, aren't we?" he yells into her ear. "You don't need to show off in front of us."

She is embarrassed and scared but mostly angry. There's nothing to say. She turns to him and gives him the finger.

"Hamska natura." He pushes her.

Andrzej the drummer blocks her fall but doesn't help her. She straightens. The full band, four of them sweaty and tall around her, are menacing; but mostly it's Marek who scares her.

She takes a half-step toward him. "Huj," she spits it out, turns and moves quickly toward the door. When she's outside, she runs.

The city centre feels bare and strange. The tall buildings are not unlike downtown Edmonton. At a small Chinese food stand with tiny white tables outside, she stops by and sits down. The clerk's Chinese; the woman and Baska point to the menu above. When a styrofoam container containing vegetables, chicken and noodles arrives, she is relieved. As she eats, she pulls out her map. A block down, a small neon sign advertising "girls" isn't reassuring. Walking out of the metro here at night and getting home might be all right, but casually strolling by yourself probably isn't.

All Baska wants to do is have a fucking good cry. The obscenities etched into the plastic table remind her of the graffiti in her high-school bathroom: *Eat shit, 20 million Polacks can't be wrong.* She covers the word *gowno* with her hand. She cannot imagine what Marek could have heard or seen in New York, or why he got so angry with her. Baska looks at the Asian clerk and wonders what racist shit she must hear here, in Warsaw, everyday.

But Baska knows she is only two or three blocks away from the lights of the Old Town and if she stays on Swietokrzyska, and heads east, she'll reach Nowy Swiat eventually. Safe. So she throws the remainder of her food away and leaves.

When she reaches the park by Smolna, an old man on the bench calls to her. He looks drunk.

"I have no money," she tells him.

"Well then if you don't have any money, you must have time to listen to a joke." He's smiling.

"Okay, I'll take a free joke."

"A father bought his five-year-old son a choochoo train, Jasiu (that's the name of the son) having ridden on Warsaw trams with his mom was used to hearing 'kurwa mac, wsiadac i cicho siedziec (get the fuck on and be quiet.)' So every time the boy played with the train he'd say the same thing. When his father heard this he made Jasiu kneel in the corner. But the next time Jasiu played *driver* he said the same thing again, so his father made him kneel in the corner again. And again. Finally Jasiu's mother intervened. So his father got Jasiu to promise not to repeat that phrase and let him play with the train. When his father left the room, Jasiu turned to his mother and said, 'Myslalem ze ten huj nigdy nie wysiadzie (I thought that bastard would never get off.)'"

Baska laughs.

"See, I made you laugh. I guess that's pretty good too."

She nods. "Thanks." She crosses the park and walks toward her hostel.

HOW CAN ONE LEAVE? (FROM THE UNOFFICIAL COURTSHIP OF TERESKA ROGOWSKA: KIETRZ, 1968) "Hey, excuse me, from what division are you?" Helen, one of Tereska's friends, asks one of the soldiers walking by the tank. Tereska smiles at the silly sign on the vehicle. She wonders if something like that is on Janek's, *Zolnierz dziewczynie nie sklamnie* (Soldier won't lie to a girl). "69th? Really? Her boyfriend is in that division."

"What's his name?" the soldier asks.

"Janek, Jan R——," Tereska says.

"No? Yeah. Corporal R——? He's sleeping. I'll wake him up for you." The soldier smiles at her and Helen. He jumps onto the tank and opening the hatch he disappears inside. The soldier walking on the other side comes over to them, talks up Helen.

Janek appears up from the top. He looks sleepy. As he lifts himself up and out, he appears even slimmer than she remembers him. He rubs his shaved head and adjusts his beret. "I didn't know we'd be passing through Kietrz..." he says.

She thinks, typical. It may be months before they see each other again and he.... But the way he jumps down, steps up to her, and looks down, as if he could eat her up with his eyes, she doesn't say anything.

"We're going to Czechoslovakia...."

"I know," she says.

"I bet that's all they really need down there."

"You're helping save Czechoslovakia from the threatening western influence. Saving socialism...." Tereska tries to joke but it's not in her.

"I can't believe they're not telling us anything. Fucking communist bastards, always lying to us...."

"Janek...."

"It's just like an exercise...."

"I know. When we went to Warsaw, we danced in front of Gomulka at the Stadium near Praga. Warsaw is beautiful. Is Toronto like Warsaw?"

"No. It's better, it's different," he tells her.

"I can't imagine that...."

"The city spreads right into Lake Ontario. It's cleaner than the Baltic Sea, you can go swimming and fishing all summer long. And play hockey in winter."

"Janek...."

"What?"

"I'm not sure what I'd do there...."

"But there's no future here. We'll buy a car and travel the whole country: Canada's as big as eight Polands." He puts his arms around her, "Once you see it, you'll never want to come back."

Tereska's almost glad when he lets her go and she's left standing by herself, watching the armored cars and soldiers walking past. She's not sentimental; she's practical. But she's only nineteen. She looks down at her shoes...sees a scuff. A children's song gets in her head: *Skacze wrobel po desce szyje buty Teresce, Tereska sie raduje nowe buty obuje. Nie raduj sie Tereska bo te buty dla pieska. (A sparrow jumps on wood, sewing shoes for Tereska. Tereska's delighted she's getting new shoes. But Tereska don't be happy those shoes are for your puppy.)* It's a silly song; makes Tereska suddenly feel sad....

HOW WILL YOU LEAVE WARSAW? (1 AUGUST, 2001) Baska buys a candle and places it at the monument to the Warsaw Uprising. The striking colour of the greenish blue wall, opposite, lightens the fierce sculpture of the partisans. A man with two children approaches the monument. She watches them while they light their candles. The man seems a little tipsy and younger than he appeared from afar. She wonders at the children with him: the boy and girl look nine and ten years old. "Where are you from?" he asks.

"Kietrz," she tells him, "niedaleko od Opola."

"I'm from Sandomierz. I brought my niece and nephew to Warsaw. You know with the Warsaw uprising and the summer vacation."

"Yes," she smiles. "And my mom's birthday."

"Yours too?" he asks and she laughs although she doesn't believe him. Something about him feels too familiar. The children continue to re-light the candles while Baska and the man watch them. At times, he looks back at her and beams an inebriated smile. The smile probably has more to do with alcohol than her. Even so, she feels flattered. She wonders if one could get comfortable, like this. Then the rain begins to pour down, and she runs for a doorway of the nearby building.

When the man with the children walks past her, he says, "We're heading that way." Tipping his head to the left he asks, "Do you want to share our umbrella?"

She shakes her head although the offer feels acceptable, like in some other life she's walking off with him. "I'm going the other way."

He shrugs.

Her baggage is at the Central Train Station and she needs to head in that general direction. But there are two hours before she's to catch her train. When the rain stops, she begins walking toward the Palace of Culture and Science. As she crosses Marszalkowska, she sees a van turn and stares. She recognizes the Chinese couple from the booth where she bought her noodles. She trips on her feet.

At the Palace, instead of the silence she encountered the day before, there are two busloads of tourists. One of their guides and the nearest one to Baska is a blond, fiercely friendly woman. "Once described as 'a stone layer cake of abomination' by one of Warsaw's most prominent writers, Tadeusz Konwicki, the Palace has always attracted controversy," she says. The tour group moves toward the entrance of the building where a couple dressed in traditional Polish costumes welcomes them and breaks into, of all dances, Krakowiak. Baska slips into the tour group unnoticed and watches, just as she has done all week in galleries and museums. When the dancers finish and the tourists disappear into the Palace, Baska remains and sits down by the fountain.

A priest is sitting opposite her. With his feet in the water, he's absorbed in the book he's reading. Baska keeps him within her peripheral vision as she watches the two dancers. The girl pulls her colourful, hand-sewn skirt high up around her waist and from a pair of cotton shorts she takes out a pack of cigarettes. Her skirt is folded out of harm's way as she sits smoking her cigarette awaiting the next group of tourists. The man beside her takes a drink from a bottle, spitting, squirting out the last mouthful on the steps. To Baska, this stream is a river, a question: **WILL YOU COME BACK?**

J. M. VILLAVERDE

Dance of the Suitors

Talking on the phone about things that brought us together instead of pulling us apart, we got to agreeing that the time had come again to pay a visit. We split it evenly, Angela would do the paying and I would do the visiting. She booked the flight, the ticket was waiting for me at check-in, and I flew down on a rainy Friday in May.

This was usually a short flight. The cabin was like a cramped classroom and full of stripes, ties and pink newspapers. I overheard voices muttering about markets and their mood swings. I heard puzzling combinations of letters in groupings of three or four, which resolved into ticker symbols. Across the aisle sat a man who looked any age in a wide range. A youthful 40, a mature 20. He held a textbook in his lap, a chewed-up straw between his lips. He was absorbing the basics of marketing. I put my head against the glass and tried to recapture the ecstasy of flight, some shred of it. The plane's vibrations travelled through me, mincing the conversations. I declined the snack and even the drink. I kept my head against the window and my eyes in the clouds. After a while I took a pill, let it nest awhile under my tongue. It was quite legal and I'd say what it was, but where's the poetry in a short chemical-sounding name? I swallowed it, and the effect was almost immediate. Around me a net of loose threads began to spread.

There was cloud cover all the way to Boston. This seemed like a sign I decided not to interpret. We circled Logan until a runway opened up. The plane spilled us onto the tarmac and a bus ferried us to the terminal. We were surrounded by a cold mist, a wet chill. The pavement gleamed with it.

She was waiting by the baggage carousel. Turning but empty. She smiled when she saw me, and I felt myself ignite. We kissed on the mouth, we'd always done that. We held each other like trying to recapture something. Angela led me back to her car. It was parked illegally, both flashers blinking, but we got to it before the cop did.

The rain began again. We drove through it. I turned and watched her.

"What are you doing?" she said. "Studying my profile? Is my nose getting longer? My chin sagging?"

"Stop it."

Angela was homing in on 40 without appearing to. She had plain good looks, which she managed like a retirement fund. Thirty-eight and the blush was still there. I continued to look at her until a smile crept in. She gave me one of those sidelong glances I sometimes see even when she's not around. I sat there in her new car measuring how much I'd missed Angela, how much I missed my darling twin sister, the apple of our parents' eye, and mine.

Here I was in another city, another country, embarking on a long weekend of planned events. She had described them on the phone. A dinner party, a special brunch. Even the evening of my arrival was booked. Usually my weekends were empty and shapeless, I moved through them unimpeded.

"We're going back to my place first," she said. "There's enough time."

I nodded. Angela knew this meant I'd forgotten where we were supposed to go after going to her place first. She reminded me. She'd arranged for us to attend a ceremony for graduating psychoanalysts; it was being held, this year, at Wellesley College. Why were we spending a rainy but otherwise perfectly fine Friday evening in this way? She had just started attending the local chapter of the psychoanalytic institute and wanted a preview of her own graduation, which she calculated was seven years away. Seven years. When I think about her perseverance I wonder if we're really related.

Angela was neat. In her apartment she arranged things.

Just so. She lived in one of a cluster of well-barbered suburbs. Impeccable lawns, well-swept landscapes, and every once in a while a flag. I asked what it was like living on a golf course. Her eyes stayed on the road and mine on her.

"It's like living on a golf course," she said, which translated loosely as "Don't start."

Stepping inside I paused to darken her doorway.

"Don't make yourself too comfortable." She dropped her purse on an armchair and her keys on the purse. "We're leaving soon. I'm just going to take a quick shower."

"A shower?"

"I went to the airport directly from work."

I scanned the spines of her CDs, but nothing fit the mood, whatever it was. I moved through the rooms like a perfect stranger. I didn't turn on any lights. The shower was echoing the rain. Next I was in the kitchen drinking a beer from her fridge. I leaned against the counter, a quiet room in a quiet street, my stomach empty and my senses thickening between sips. I was aware of dark hallways and empty rooms. Angela lived in an apartment too large for a single person, which was what she was. She never talked about finding *the one*, settling down, starting a family. She showed no sign of hearing the clock ticking. When she came out of the bathroom she was caught momentarily in a wedge of light as she moved to the bedroom. She was wearing underwear with a faded floral pattern and a towel like a cape. My breath caught on the breasts (small) and nipples (alert) and the twin swells of flesh hipside. A moment of cinematic perfection instantly dissolved.

In the car again, my thoughts zooming along with it.

"You should be paying more attention to the directions," Angela said. "They're very precise, and I don't want to get lost."

I brought the piece of paper in my lap into focus. A long

list of turns and stoplights, exits and more turns. There was even a hand-drawn map of the campus.

"Talk to me," she said.

"You have to get on the Mass Pike."

"Okay, but talk to me."

We shared the love twins share, tempered by distance. We argued about things, a list of them, our parents at the top. In later life they'd decided to spice up their marriage by vandalizing it. They fought now, which they hadn't before, about the past, diverging recollections. These were dwarfish antagonisms, disagreements, minor stuff. Angela didn't agree. "I talk to them," she said, meaning Mum, "more than you do. I know the situation, and it's serious." But it was of little interest to me, and this paragraph was all it was getting.

We talked about family, nothing argument-provoking, our older brother and sister. It wasn't a long conversation. Angela had zero news and I had roughly the same. Karen and Russell had both crossed over into their forties, and no-one made any noise about it. They both lived abroad. So did Angela, come to think of it, but they had crossed an ocean. Karen was living in Toulouse with her third French husband. She liked their return policy, she used to joke. As for Russell, he was with a prestigious investment firm in London whose top performer was a dart-throwing monkey.

She glanced at me and tried again, "How are you?"

"How am I?"

"Is that too general? Should I ask a more specific question? Yes? No?"

"Whatever you like," I said.

"How's work?"

"No questions about work. I don't want you falling asleep at the wheel."

"How's your love life?"

I hated that expression, mainly for its inaccuracy. What love has is a half-life.

69

"You don't have to tell me if you don't want to."

But I did. I wanted to tell her something. I told her about a recent date. The night before, actually. A lecturer at the university. She and I were the only non-Russians in the Russian department. She was about my age, her loneliness exerted some force over me, both push and pull. That was the story I told Angela, instead of telling her that my girlfriend of two years was getting a divorce, and I was getting harder to reach on the phone.

We found Wellesley without trouble. It was a green town, every possible shade, mostly currency-green. The place shone, even in the rain it looked buffed. The pinpoint directions led us to the College. Also to the "x" on the map—the building where the event was being held. We circled it a couple of times before we saw a parking spot (not indicated in our otherwise irreproachable directions).

The ceremony was already under way. Someone ushered us into a conference hall and pointed to two empty chairs in back, the farthest point from the podium. It was now officially a full house. As soon as she sat, Angela beamed her concentration on the speaker. I discovered that psychoanalysts are like other professionals—they make funny speeches. I scanned the room for something—some hook, some peg—to hang my attention on.

A matron materialized in front of me. She was holding a tray.

"Oh, yes," I almost said. I took two glasses and gave my sister one. We drank the champagne stand-in to the graduates, to their success. A voice at the other end of the room invited us to cross the hallway into a smaller room where they were keeping the food.

"You go ahead," Angela said. "I have to talk to someone."

I joined a line leading to a vast still life of fruit, ham and cake. It occurred to me that I'd forgotten to ask myself what I was doing there. Across the buffet table, directly across, was where I first saw the girl. Everyone in the room wore a name tag except for her. She stood surveying serving dish after serving dish. She looked up and bumped into my gaze. Eyes as dark as her hair and her dress. It made the whiteness of her skin seem like a kind of provocation that couldn't go unanswered. Instead, I turned to the food and let her work her way out of the room. Who was she? I wondered. More important, where was Angela?

Angela was sitting in the middle of the conference hall. There were three men at her table. I was sure I knew who they were. She had told me about them on the phone. Three well-regarded colleagues with an interest in my sister. Mentors, or would-be, with ten years on her. Also, born-again bachelors. Three suitors all at once, and in the same room. This had to be a first. She'd done well to change cities. In Boston, Angela stood out; in Montreal, more a catwalk than a city on sunny days, who took any notice? They were talking shop, a perfect excuse for swerving. But Angela's look brought me in for a landing, and I sat next to her.

She introduced us to one another but the only name that stayed with me was my own. All three seemed relieved to learn I was her brother. It gave them permission to dismiss me. They didn't even raise an eyebrow at the word "twin" these shrinks. I sat back for a panoramic view.

They spoke in a mix of New England Ease and psychopharmacological argot. There were polished, participle-laden sentences. One of the suitors was more impressive than the others; he was supremely bald and wore a regal air of entitlement.

"Are you considering the job at McLean?" he said.

"I'm thinking about it," Angela said in a tone hinting she was thinking about everything but.

"It would be wonderful to have you onside."

None of them seemed interested in joining the food line, but I can report that my cooked ham and cold sauerkraut were excellent. Each suitor leaned over the table in Angela's direction and leaned back when he realized the other two were doing it. Their bodies spoke for them—their language gave nothing away. Their range of facial expressions hinted at advanced robotics. I began to scan the room for a particular black dress.

Dancing followed dining. With intervals for drinking. A Cuban band was playing on the second floor, Salsa, Rumba and such. There was a bar at the opposite end, and a bartender young enough to be a long-lost son. There were three brands of gin, he might've been conducting a taste test. I asked for a g and t; I got a puzzled look instead. Then I took my spelled-out drink for a tour of the room. Angela seemed to be taking turns talking to each of the suitors, maybe she was conducting her own test. It was only when she was speaking with suitor number three that I began to pay more attention. I realized I wasn't being vigilant enough. Her demeanour was different from when she faced all three; now she was the one leaning forward.

I directed my steps to the edge of the dance floor. When I looked over my shoulder, I saw that girl again. She had a pale angular face, a face belonging to someone with famine in her family history. She was standing by the bar with a glass of white wine in her right hand. Her left hand she used to keep her hair out of her eyes. She was conversing with the bartender (a mesmerized fringe of blond curls, not old enough to drink what he was serving).

By the time I went for another drink she was on the dance floor. Swaying on her own like an apparition. Something about her was keeping the men away. I put my glass down and got in there. She smiled like she'd been waiting for me (I didn't ask her to confirm this).

"You're not wearing a name tag," she said.

I recognized her. Like me she was an interloper. With, I was certain, a connection to the psychoanalytic world more tenuous even than mine. I looked round for proprietary eyes and lost interest in mid-sweep. We were all grownups here, of all places, I might've reasoned. She spoke with an accent, something Eastern European, glottal waves lapping up against the shores of the Black Sea. As with so much else, I wasn't going to be like everyone else, I wasn't going to ask. She was going to tell me where she was from, if and when. She wore mystery like a tailored garment, and I both wanted and didn't want to undress her. I did ask her name though. "Maryna," she said, which seemed to fit.

"What do you do?"

"I teach Russian," she said.

"Of course," I almost said. My life was full of lazy coincidences.

I wanted to hear more about her.

"You first," she said.

Now I didn't hesitate. I described my brief career as a spoken-word artist. At the time I was deep in my twenties, firmly entrenched. Performances were held in coffeehouses and bars, the darker the better. I recited things that were trance-inducing and I'd fall under my own spell. I remembered it as a time of consummate derangement. The words would come, incoherent, hallucinatory, visionary. They spilled out of me. I had no control over it, my dreaming tongue.

The rest of the time, days on end, I hardly said a word. I didn't have to keep my mouth shut, or even try. I had a talent for silence, I had a talent for silences.

"You seem to have lost it," Maryna said. "Lucky for me, I guess."

Angela was on the dance floor. She'd been dancing with someone but when I looked again he was gone. Now she was surrounded by her three suitors, and no exit. They were swaying around her, exhibiting the adhesive properties of a shower curtain. They seemed unaware of the comical effect they were producing, the faces they lit up around them. It was a Camcorder moment. For the tiniest fraction of a second our eyes met, Angela's and mine.

I turned back to Maryna and liked the smile I saw.

"She's the one you came with."

"My sister."

"I have eyes," she said.

Among other things.

I stepped closer and placed my forearm on her back as if the band had switched to a slow number. Her smile grew brighter, and seemed to turn into Angela's cue. My sister glided over and gently reclaimed me. For a magical moment the three suitors were left dancing on their own. They watched Angela slip away and stopped swaying and moving their limbs like machines winding down. They evil-eyed one another and broke into a scuffle. For a second it looked like it could go anywhere, but embarrassment immediately extinguished it. Then they walked off in different directions. I noticed that Maryna had performed her own magic—a disappearing act.

"Are you looking at them?" Angela asked. "Or are you looking for her?"

Angela shone. My own private sun. Of course, I was being unfair when I said who took notice of her in our hometown. Who didn't? Angela was the equal of any beauty parading along St. Catherine Street and had what they lacked—star quality. She was smiling now, high on attention. I basked in the microclimate of her mood. Somehow I caught the most fleeting glimpse of Maryna going to the bar, arm in arm with some guy, a mere shadow next to her. Finally, the band switched to a slower number, and I drew Angela in, her head resting on my shoulder. Now someone could've gone and dimmed the lights.

Tatyana's House

I was spending summer like small change riding the bus to a school an hour away. Five days a week in a classroom getting reacquainted with Russian. Language and culture. Eight students in all, the sons and daughters of Russian immigrants, refugees, defectors. Or grandsons and granddaughters. All except one—sometimes they still asked what I was doing there. I was also the youngest, but not by much. I was fifteen, on the dot.

Despite exalted grades this wasn't the first year I attended summer school. For some reason, buses were always involved. They padlocked the local high school from June to September. Through the window I watched it all file past, the streets and vacant lots of the suburb where I lived. Too hideous to name. I let it all slide out of focus and settled on some middle distance where I found conjugating Russian verbs easier. Things stayed out of focus until I saw a hand waving in front of me, close enough to bite. It was followed by Desmond's voice. "Anyone home?" it said. Somehow he'd been cast as my best friend, and all summer long we rehearsed our lines.

I loved riding this particular bus. It was old and about to fall apart. I wondered if we'd be on it when it happened. Every few blocks it stopped for a pick-up. Whenever the driver's foot met the brake pedal or the accelerator, a tremor went through us. I waited for it. Every morning kids got on the bus in the same sequence and sat in the same seats. There, they were doing it again. The whole thing seemed ordained. I pulled a notebook out of my bag and finished my homework. Irregular verbs. Around me, a dozen conversations were scattering like light.

From across the aisle Pamela turned in my direction. I'd talked to her before, but never for long. She was studying something just beyond me, out the window, as if trying to memorize it. Her mouth was slightly open, her moist lower lip hanging out to dry. A bubble of blondness surrounded her like atmosphere. Her eyes dared you to guess their colour. I felt my teeth digging into my lower lip. Without warning Pamela refocused. Her eyes fell on mine with a thud I couldn't believe no-one'd heard. Mine slid helplessly off. And just kept falling. I'm thinking, I'm thinking, if I let it, shyness will crush me.

Next comes the school. A sprawling structure, the colour of oatmeal, squat and window-anemic. We were pulling in a little early. I was trying to stay with those verbs, but there were too many other things calling out to me. For example, it was early morning, it was June, the air so crisp it crunched. A morning veined with sunlight. Where I lived the weather always called attention to itself.

Desmond got off the bus before I did and was, not a minute later, talking to Pamela. Let him. My throat was dry. Something he said made her laugh. I pictured the water fountains indoors, then somehow I was indoors, quenching. I got chewing gum in a shiny wrapper out of a coin machine. I was turning fifteen—did I mention that?—an excellent student, a quick study. But a laggard in other departments. When it came to relating to others I was a step behind. Conversation friendship dating. It was all shrouded in mystery, like the Great Pyramids or the Bermuda Triangle. It was supposed to be like learning your native language or learning to walk. It was supposed to be that easy.

I walked by the chemistry and biology labs. Wooden benches and gleaming, black countertops, perfect for carving things into with my house key. These classrooms looked like rooms in other schools, in my own school, in the school in the city where my mother taught biology to kids my age.

A bell was ringing. Insistent, annoying. This wasn't where I wanted to be, a fluo-lit hallway leading to a win-

76

dowless classroom. This wasn't it. But what was? My homework was done, my Russian conjugations impeccable. I was
prepared for the surprise quiz Mr. Markov announced he
would spring on us. But I didn't want it, didn't want to feel
what I was feeling, whatever it was. I wondered what
Desmond was doing. I saw that the door to my classroom
was closed. And then I saw Desmond, heading in my direction, flashing a smile like a silver badge. He was on his way
to his lesson in algebra. My hand was turning the doorknob,
pushing, the door giving way. As he skipped by Desmond
said something. It seemed out of synch with his lips. I was
turning away from him, already scanning the opening
between door and frame, the blackboard up ahead, chalky
Cyrillic inscriptions, Mr. Markov standing there, filling a
characteristic pose. I heard what Desmond said as I let go of
the door.

"She likes you."

What he said left an echo. You didn't automatically believe
what Desmond said. He was half-experiencer, half-experi-
menter. It's the second part that worried me. He liked to set
up situations, stand back, and watch it all unfold.
Sometimes accomplices were involved. You listened to what
he had to say—because how could you not?—but then you
stepped softly in the knowledge that the floor might give
out under your feet. Which reminds me. Desmond was like
the house he lived in. It was sparsely furnished and in the
washroom the bathtub was missing. Instead of one, there
was a rectangular opening through which you could see part
of the basement. That view gave me a creepy feeling. Also,
what were you supposed to do if you felt like a bath?

There was something else missing from his house.
Parents. He claimed to have a complete set but I never saw
them. He would ask me to come over, I always found the
front door unlocked. Through the opening where the bathtub should've been I once saw Desmond and a girl I'd never

seen before, or ever saw again, on the basement couch. It struck me that the couch hadn't been there the time before. Their mouths were welded in a kiss. For a moment nothing moved. Their mouths began to work, it was like a close-up, and on the soundtrack, sounds like wet slaps. The thought of it now made me chew harder. Mr. Markov suggested I get rid of my gum. His request had a certain ring to it, it sounded like repeated speech. I met his gaze and he resorted to Russian. Mr. Markov insisted on decorum in his classroom, the way my father did at home. "Da," I said and lobbed it into the trash bin without using my hands.

In the first class he'd held a getting-to-know-you session. We had to say something about ourselves and explain our interest in Russian language and culture. They all climbed up their family tree. For a moment I considered inventing a Tsarist ancestor but I immediately saw the lie was going to require too much effort to sustain. It was a flash of insight, the kind that makes you pleased with yourself. Mr. Markov asked why I was smiling. I said I was trying not to, and he didn't pursue it. When it was his turn he told us he had a passion for teaching. He taught us the word for it—actually, both words, passion and teaching as well as their intricate etymologies. I yearned for a window. The day stretched out before us like the steppes in the posters hanging by the blackboard.

I waited for the school bus to take me back. It was afternoon, past two, past three, the air bloated with sunlight. Morning and afternoon were like different seasons, indescribable mutations in the sky, I won't mention the weather again. There were occasions when Desmond and I would take another bus after school—a city bus. This one crossed the river to a driving range where we would spend an hour. Usually, I sprayed the field in every direction with golf balls while he effortlessly produced straight-ahead drives. Clearly, he'd been getting in some practice time without me.

Sometimes, I would just watch as he sent them sailing nearly 200 yards.

In three years Desmond had come a long way. The transformation was radical. Things had disappeared forever from his locker, the science fiction and fantasy paperbacks, the packed lunches, the magnetized chess set. Things had disappeared from his face, the glasses and the delicate fuzz above his lip. I liked those afternoons on the city bus, on the driving range. I enjoyed those afternoons, but this wasn't one of them. Desmond wasn't even around when the school bus arrived.

For the ride back we sat wherever. We had a new bus and a new driver, no explanations offered. Pamela was the last one to get on, she sat near the front. Suddenly, Desmond's absence was puzzling. The door closed with a hydraulic whoosh. The bus pulled away from the curb so smoothly it hardly felt like motion. Sitting next to me, Paul Kuznetsov was describing something that had happened in class until his voice began to blend in with the background noise. The bus was sailing, it was gliding. Occasionally, I looked in Pamela's direction. It wasn't mutual. They say if you stare at the back of someone's head long enough... Well, they said so many things. I noticed that I missed our old bus's death rattle.

When I got home, our next-door neighbours were sitting on their porch. They were all out there. The Schmidts, who were and looked retired, their son Helmut, and Tatyana (his wife). They waved or smiled as I walked by. Tatyana said hello in Russian. The Schmidts made guttural sounds, made it sound effortless, Helmut occasionally translating from his parents' German into English for Tatyana.

I went inside and down the stairs. Somewhere in the house Bunter was barking his fool head off. I shared the basement bedroom with my brother. My sisters' bedrooms were on the second floor, each her own. Karen was seventeen and acted 24 and Angela was my twin. I sat in my room and wondered what to do with the rest of the afternoon. I called Bunter and took him for a run in the park.

After supper, Dad brought out a store-bought cake that was capsizing. It sat in the middle of the table, unencumbered by the 30 candles he had decided would be impractical. Fifteen for Angela, the same for me. They all sang happy birthday, even Doreen, my brother's girlfriend, whom I hardly ever saw because I hardly ever saw Russell. The fact that it was my birthday didn't get me out of doing the dishes. Rules were rules and Thursday was my day.

When the last plate, the last utensil was washed and dried and returned to its proper cupboard or drawer, I joined my siblings and Doreen in the living-room. They were watching a sitcom. I read the movie summaries in the TV schedule that came in the Saturday paper. I liked movies and had finally figured out you were supposed to take your cues from them. Dad walked in and turned the volume down. He handed the remote control to one of us and left the house. I sensed more than saw the look Karen and Russell exchanged. Actually, he'd done this before. We'd wondered why he cared if the TV was on too loud if he was leaving the house. Russell said, "It's his house," meaning he never really left it. Either that or Dad was conducting an experiment, conditioning our behaviour, although that would've been more our mother's department.

"How about taking us out for ice cream for our birthday?" Angela said.

"Let's do it," Russell said, and we were suddenly on the move.

Count on Angela to mobilize us, it was something she did. She was a catalyst. She was also the reason I attended summer school. We finished each other's sentences and we fought. The littlest things set her off, and she knew how to throw my switch, too. We shared the affection twins share, magnified by the difference in gender. We turned fraternal love into something demonstrative, inventive. It worried our parents and they devised a plan. We began to attend different schools, and I got used to year-round bussing. Now I was going to summer school during the day and Angela babysat most evenings. She was employed by three young families on our street. All three husbands took a particular interest in her was what it looked like. Something about Angela, though, she could handle herself. Except when I was around.

We sat there spooning it up from paper cups, except for Doreen who'd ordered a cone. I tried to keep my hair out of my ice cream, brushed it away from my eyes. Again it fell like a curtain. It was thick wavy blue-black and abundant. It was inexhaustible. My brother's girlfriend ran her hand through it and asked if I'd like to swap.

"Your brother's prettier than I am," she said to my brother.

Doreen's hair was straight and thin, the same red as her freckles or my blushing face. Russell's was also thin, thinning, he'd only just turned twenty.

I sat at the top of the basement stairs. I felt the cold marble step through my pyjamas. My parents were in the living-room, having a conversation. I heard snippets I was piecing together. If they'd been in the dining-room, they would've been out of earshot. I would've had to get closer and risk getting caught. I loved to sit there listening.

There were times when my eavesdropping was interrupted by my sleepwalking brother. One night a couple of months earlier he had tried to leave the house and struggled with the lock until my father steered him back to our room. My brother was aware of his sleepwalking. He told me once that sleepwalkers are lucid. He looked up to see if I knew what the word meant and saw mostly the whites of my eyes.

"Sleepwalkers know exactly what they're doing," he said, so forcefully I wanted to believe it. Many of these episodes he claimed to relive as flashbacks. I didn't roll my eyes when he said stuff like that.

"Your son can't take his eyes off Tatyana," my mother was saying.

There was a silence. It was almost as if I could hear my dad smiling. Finally, he said, "Has Doreen caught him at it?"

"I'm talking about your other son."

"Really? Well, it's about time he took an interest in girls."

"Tatyana is no girl," she said, her tone almost accusing. "She's a married woman."

I couldn't believe this conversation. It was like a hike in my allowance. I went to bed elated. My mother's observation about Tatyana, about me, felt like a discovery. It was as if a door I didn't even know existed had swung open.

2

This part is about visions. I wanted them. Wanted them without resorting to drugs, though I wasn't ruling anything out. Visions like lucid dreams. I wanted to succumb to them.

There was a small room next to the kitchen that served as my father's study. It was a cozy place with a lining of book spines. In it he shuttled between desk and armchair. In boxes in the closet were old-fashioned photo albums with evidence of parental travel. There were also reels of Super-8 film but no projector. I held them up to the light. Layers of dust on everything until I came along. In those boxes I saw places that were gone now, faces too, and my own hometown in disguise.

My father's study was his sanctuary; it was where he went to feed his prose habit. I wandered in once, some unguarded Sunday, and came out a little different. In his study I found the novels and verse he read and reread. There were books piled on a table. In them a variety of bookmarks with international addresses, in some cases the last reminders, my dad told me, of vanished bookshops. I read the poets on his shelves, things we didn't cover in English class. I read biographical blurbs on yellowing dust jackets. I was drawn to these poets, the madder the better. And suicides were best of all. They left strange words that called to me. And they seemed to be aware of their power. I read them again and again, making connections I almost blamed myself for not seeing before. That was what I wanted: to see. I had a thirst for visions and a special destined feeling I fed like an ulcer. I was in training for the thing I would become, a dreamer, a fantasist.

When Tatyana sat on the porch in a revealing T-shirt or tight sweater was when boys my age who lived up the street would turn up at our door. Could I come out and play? Who ordinarily wanted nothing to do with me. "Come back a little later," I'd say. They walked away and I timed the beginning of a porch-to-porch conversation with Tatyana to coincide with their first backward glance. We usually talked about writing. She was studying English. "Specializing," she said, "in writing with creativity." Her English constructions sounded experimental and her fractured grammar sang to me. We talked about her writing and we talked about mine. What I'd shown her were the first three chapters of a murder mystery without, I was sure, the least merit. These were long chapters, nearly 60 pages in all, containing probably more than a third of the whole story, and there wasn't the slightest hint of mystery or murder in there yet. The hero was a detective named Dumfries, a Scotsman resettled in California. Back in Glasgow he'd lost his wife and some motor skills to a stray bullet of all things. How I came up with this stuff I couldn't say, though plagiarism springs to mind.

It wasn't long before I was lifting lines from my suicidal poets. Borrowing them, actually, trying them on to see if they fit. Phrases images ideas—I would disassemble and reassemble them. I showed this stuff to Tatyana. She called it poetry and liked it better than the crippled Scot. She found things to say about it, not always praise, not nearly, and kept finding things to say. It was all the encouragement I needed.

Like you, I expected Desmond to mention Pamela again. To ask me if I'd spoken to her. Was I, in other words, taking part in his latest experiment? What he did instead was tell me about a girl he'd been with the night before. We were at the driving range. He'd emptied his bucket of balls and was starting in on mine. What he said reminded me of something I'd heard before. A few months earlier, my brother had taken a job at a big plumbing supplies company where he was involved in stock-keeping. Ask him what he'd done at work and he would recite product codes and quantities. Desmond's story sounded like that, an inventory of the girl's assets. I didn't catch her name, maybe he didn't offer it. I was hearing a detailed anatomy lesson. Desmond's tone was detached. It triggered another memory, my mind wouldn't keep still. One evening—maybe I was nine, maybe ten—my mother had led me from my room to the living-room. She made me sit in the armchair and sat down on the edge of the footrest. A matching footrest, I noticed again, its leather faded in the soft light. It was as if the scene had been set, the props put in place. It must've been a Sunday, it had the feel of a Sunday. Snow was falling in pillowy flakes. There was a glow from the fireplace that lit the room with a kind of anticipation. My mother began. She presented the facts about sex clinically, and gently, like detaching muscle from bone without damaging the sinews. Then came question period—she asked all the questions. Had I heard something like this from my friends? How was I getting on with the girls at school? Did I like any one in particular?

Desmond did something he always he did. He changed the subject completely. You couldn't go back, ask for clarification, ask what her name was, this girl so minutely itemized. He had no use for transitions. He asked me what I hadn't expected. Could he read the novel I was writing? I must've mentioned it to him. Could he read my novel-in-progress, that was what he called it.

I looked at him. Blankly, I guess.

"Can I read it?" he said, this time allowing it to sound more like a question.

Only one person had read what I'd written. And Tatyana knew she was the only one.

It was Sunday morning, no school, Russian homework that could wait till I was on the bus again. My mother went next door with something she'd baked and came back with it. "I guess they've gone to church," she said. The Schmidts, their son, even that Tatyana.

I called Bunter. Walking him was a job I shared with Dad. Bunter, you should know, wasn't spayed. Most times he ran around the park and returned when you called; every so often, he'd run off and you could call and call. He would come back two days later, smiling. One time, he returned missing an ear but still smiling. On the way back from the park I noticed that both cars—the Schmidts' nondescript sedan (or station-wagon) and their son's scrap-yard special— were back in the driveway next door. If they'd all gone to church together, they wouldn't've taken two cars, that was what occurred to me. Idle thoughts leading nowhere.

If Helmut had a job, it seemed to elude description. Their bedroom like mine was in the basement. Why were they living with Helmut's parents? Were they saving for a home of their own? Were they on their way to someplace else? Questions I didn't try to answer because they occurred to me only much later. What I knew about them I could put into a haiku. He was job-hunting. Better prospects, a move up. And he would get it.

Of course, wherever he went, Tatyana would follow. She would go. The job could be in another part of town or in another country—the result would be the same.

How did I know they would leave? From sitting at the top of the stairs on the cold step tuning my parents in. The subject was a trip the Schmidts were planning; the destination surprised me.

"Who'd want to go to Winnipeg?" I asked myself. For a moment I thought I'd said that out loud. I held my breath and waited for an answer. It turned out the Schmidts were going to visit family out there. Family with serious business interests. It took one more visit to the top of the stairs two nights later to find out that the Schmidts were contemplating a similar journey for Helmut.

Sunday noon. Angela was in her room, door closed, radio on. Karen and Russell were out. I sat in the living-room, looking through the TV listings for a movie to watch. As for my parents, they were in the kitchen having coffee. Discussing, again, a movie they'd seen a month before. A French film called *Get Out Your Handkerchiefs*.

Sunday afternoon. Desmond wasn't picking up the phone, no-one was, and I ended up patrolling the mall. I went from store to store, but whatever it was, it wasn't catching my attention. There was disco music blaring from the record shop. This was the seventies, the decade that wouldn't end. The light in there was flat, that was the effect it had on me. The mall was where it was happening, except for this particular one. Across the street from the mall was the recreation complex with its arcades, bowling alley, flea market, and pimply faced pushers.

I saw Pamela. She was moving through the mall quickly. There was someone with her. A girlfriend? Not someone I'd seen before. She trailed Pamela like hired help. In every shop

86

Pamela picked things up and dropped them almost immediately. I got close enough to see her thumbs, which I'd noticed before. They started out long-stemmed and ended wider and foreshortened. They made me think of hammerhead sharks. What else? She was fifteen, not a whole week older than I. Her eyes were blue, so light they seemed to repel light. She moved from rack to clothing rack, shop to shop, never settling. I watched her, I could've counted every blond strand.

I tried to imagine following her through familiar streets to her neighbourhood, her street, her door. But impatience wouldn't let me. It made me skip ahead. I saw Pamela's house—I knew which one—I saw Pamela's room. We materialized in it. We were wearing what we'd worn at the mall. I felt pinpricks along my hands. They wanted to reach out and I wanted them to. There was an opening between shirt and jeans on her left side, which my eyes found. Then my hand. Then my elbow. Suddenly, she dipped into another shop, some clothing store.

This was the end of the line. I went to the coffee-shop next door, ordered something and sat down. I noticed that the music store wasn't blaring any more. They were pumping muzak through the whole mall like Demerol. Tatyana entered my thoughts unannounced. This happened more and more, but I didn't let on. Next thing, Pamela and her friend were taking a seat. At a table so close to mine I could smell the perfume. She glanced over. She threw glances, that was what she did. I tried to put on a look of unconcern but it was a bad fit. She was connected to her drink by a straw. Only Pamela had a shopping bag, a small one, arranged in her lap.

Pamela reached into her purse and found a cigarette. I didn't know she smoked. I was finding things out.

"You got a light?"

When her friend turned toward me I realized the question was directed at me.

87

I shook my head because I couldn't remember the words for, "Ah, no, I don't."

Pamela reached in again for a lighter. She didn't offer her friend a cigarette or even a drag. They were discussing some blouse, its colour, its price, other blouses borrowed from friends, a whole genealogy of clothing. The air in that coffee-shop should've been conditioned and maybe it was, but to me the place was equatorial. My shirt was beginning to stick to me. Pamela's cigarette burned like a long countdown.

They spoke in voices loud enough to've included me. Her friend, whose name I just remembered, kept looking over occasionally like she was preparing the ground. Finally, she spoke.

"Everyone at school thinks you're weird."

"So you know me?" Where, I wondered, did I get that glittering line.

She barked an accusation, which resolved into my name. Then she lost interest, like a blade falling.

Pamela continued to smoke her cigarette, impassive, removed. They went on with their conversation, and I was stuck there, a satellite in their orbit. Some inner voice urged me to go. Pamela put out her cigarette like she was punishing it and finished what was left of her drink. They got up to go, and this was the moment. They walked by me, side by side, their arms knotted. Pamela leaned forward as if taking aim. And she belched in my face, the loudest I'd ever heard. They skipped past me, ripples in their wake, and I began to really like her.

3

Day followed on day, summer settled in. I stood in the basement stacks, keeping from sneezing. I was looking for books at the university library that would help me write my assignment, references that weren't available at the high school library. It could've been any day in July. I was dizzy from lack of light and air. I left the dusty stacks and kept going until I was outside. The sun was shining with a kind of reproach.

The library building was a concrete structure standing on the edge of the campus; it had a façade borrowed from a previous age. A ledge girdled it, making everything above the third storey look like an afterthought. Perched on the ledge at each corner was a brass owl. They watched, unmoving. I knew from somewhere that owls signified wisdom and I guessed that these ones stood for the knowledge housed inside. I asked my father once to confirm my intuition. Their job, he said, was to keep pigeons frightened and away from the area. That's all they were, urban scarecrows.

I walked toward the old astronomy building; it was where my dad's cramped office was located. It was on the top floor next to the door that led to the observatory. The telescope was long gone. He was waiting for me. His office was a replica of the study at home, only messier, with books as the dominant life-form. There were some potted plants that thirst had turned brown. He locked the door and we rode the elevator down. As we walked across the lawn to the parking area, he pointed to the library building. Standing on an owl's head were two pigeons engaged in love play.

In the car my dad asked if I'd found what I needed. He had given me his library card and noticed I wasn't carrying any books.

"I took notes."

In a rush of vertical detachment, I saw our car from above. It was threading its way through slow-moving traffic, proceeding as in a dream. I closed my eyes. When I opened them, I was back in the passenger seat. The side mirror was tilted, framing my chin. The windshield dispersed light. The dashboard was sprinkled with it. I felt the familiar blur of motion sickness. I closed my eyes again and took a deep breath, slow and measured. When I opened them, I noticed my father's hands on the steering wheel. They seemed outsized. It was as if I were hovering on the periphery of a daydream, peering in. I felt unmoored, in two places at once, loosely enveloped in my skin and flitting above my body. There wasn't a sound, not even the car radio. More and more my father and I shared silences. They were beginning to dwarf us. His hands on the wheel were bleached with light. His skin was lined, like netting, like parchment. The march of cellular death. It was a summer day, his arms were bare. A greyish tinge seemed to claim him. My gaze travelled in repetitive strokes to his face. It bounced there, it bobbed on the edge. Briefly my eyes lit on features, one after another, lip, jaw, the tip of his nose. All of him ageing abruptly, ten more years on him, twenty. The vision squeezed a sob out of me. He asked me what was wrong. I turned and kept my eyes on the sheet of sky framed in the side window.

"I'm tired," was what occurred to me.

"Oh, come on, you can't be at your age."

It was in a dream that night that the vision was completed. During the drive he got progressively older. He became frail and I found myself behind the wheel, driving the dream to its conclusion. This time there was no view from above, no sluggish traffic. I was in it, moving faster than I thought possible. Before I knew where we were, we had arrived. We stood outside the home where I would leave him. The grounds looked landscaped and well-maintained. The building was modern, an architecture of glass and light. The only anomaly was the front door, a massive throwback made of dark, heavy wood with iron crossbars and a brass knocker. The dream ended with it swinging shut.

4

Finally, Tatyana. My mother was right, she was no girl. She was married. She was also the woman next door. Living with her husband and her in-laws at her in-laws'. Her husband's name was Helmut, a direct consequence of having German parents. They were ancient, these parents, like the continent they'd left for this bald suburb. Growing up here I dreamed of trees to climb, sturdy branches to hang tires from I could puncture with a Swiss Army knife pilfered from a classmate's locker.

This was the third summer in a row that I was taking a course in Russian. My progress was good. I could read Turgenev, Dostoyevsky, Tolstoy. The names, not the novels. Tatyana became my real connection to Russian. I didn't tell her that, I just asked for her help with my homework, even though that wasn't the kind of help I needed. That she was Russian was a coincidence. A special kind of coincidence, I learned the word looking in the dictionary for something else. Synchronicity. I had a feeling it was going to dot my life like cows in a pasture seen from a speeding train.

Tatyana was completing an MA. She was trying to finish a novel begun two years earlier. It was supposed to be her thesis and the only thing left between her and the degree. She was 24, already there was a faded quality in her face. I couldn't do anything with that beyond noticing it.

I watched her, I was like a camera around her. I didn't know what I was finding out, if anything. When Helmut was around I was even more watchful. His eyes wouldn't stay put, they'd carom off Tatyana. He spoke to her but never seemed to address her directly. When I replayed these scenes, it was as if they were on stage and I was measuring the distance between them in steps neither wanted to take.

There was no prettiness in her face, or need for it, and she wore no makeup. What she wore were blouses and T-shirts that accentuated her figure. The T-shirts were plain, never a word or an illustration printed on them. If there had been, Desmond once joked, it would've been "No vacancy." She asked me about the class. Was I liking it any better?

I didn't mean to suggest that Mr. Markov's class was always dull. He and I did what we could to liven things up. I twisted the Russian language in an effort to replay that flicker of horror on his face. I stage-whispered wrong answers to Paul Kuznetsov when the teacher sent a question his way. I kept asking, "What's the exact etymology of that word?" like a parrot cuffed with dementia.

During the regular school year, Mr. Markov taught geography. He looked like he'd been places, he'd brought back phrases in foreign languages and stories to tell. He was the main character in them, reliably bumbling and inept, and delivering high entertainment value. To prepare for trips he would read about his destinations. Unpleasant surprises still popped up. He ate things, wandered into neighbourhoods, talked to people he shouldn't have. The map wasn't the territory. "Don't forget that," he said. "It'll come in handy." On the final exam that year, he included the following question: "What is the map not?"

Desmond had asked to read my manuscript and I let him have it, a small dose, the first dozen pages. We were sitting in the cafeteria, which they kept cleaner than the one at our regular school. The place was almost full thanks to the rain. When he finished reading each page, Desmond gave it back to me. When I had a few sheets in hand I'd walk away and return to further nods, smiles, and other signs of appreciation that were directed at the page he was reading, not at me. He liked the Dumfries character and his limp. He liked the descriptions of San Francisco I got out of a dated travel guide. He didn't look up when I got up, he didn't look up when I came back. We repeated this pattern—Desmond reading and I collecting pages and ferrying them away—until he got to the last one. He stretched it, seemed to be rereading this or that sentence. When he was done with the final page he didn't hand it to me. He turned it over and laid it flat on the table with a flourish. There was a note of finality, which he held like pressing down a piano key. I didn't bother getting up this time, I tore up the sheet right in front of him.

I don't know if I expected him to say something but he didn't. He turned his head and saw the trash bin against the far wall. Some of the sheets he'd just read were jutting out like icebergs.

I made an effort to stay put. I was not going to get up before he did. I wasn't going to do that. Desmond gave me a look like he was trying to climb down my optic nerve. I saw him make the decision to smile. He reached over and picked up the torn sheet. "Let me," he said, rising. He dropped the pieces into the bin on his way out. Desmond was cool. It's what he was. And coolness, I was sure, would get him in the end.

It was Saturday afternoon, a break from school. I took a pot of leftover stew into the living-room. I perched on the arm-chair's arm, the less sagging one. Even without an audience I made it look precarious. I watched the ionized dust sparkle on the television screen. From nowhere—the bathroom actually—my father appeared. I felt captured like an incriminating snapshot. Eating in the living-room. From the pot. A ladle instead of a spoon. My feet, I noticed, were resting on the coffee table. I felt myself brace.

My father gave me a conspiratorial smile and said something unexpected. "Eating from the pot. You're going to grow up to be a bachelor."

I joined him on the porch. He was having a cigarette. My father was near the peak of his career as a smoker. I stood next to him. In the last year I'd put a spurt of growth on. It made my bones ache. I was now unexpectedly tall for my age. But I still thought of my dad as a giant. It had nothing to do with height. There was something in the way he carried himself. He crossed a room like a high-wire act. Buoyancy and tension—he meshed them. What he had was a physical signature. I saw it, others saw it, photos caught it, too.

"The Schmidts," I heard my father say and realized I was catching only the end of it, whatever it was.

"What about the Schmidts?"

This was the week they were visiting relatives in Winnipeg. They'd left the day before. I realized I'd been waiting for it.

It's where you guessed I was going and it's where I got to. It was their basement, of course, not ours. Plywood walls and a lack of clutter. Tatyana confirmed my parents' speculation. Helmut's family were trying to get him work. That was where he was now, in Winnipeg. Tatyana had heard things about the place, none enticing. We didn't dwell on it.

I started talking about Pamela. Tatyana gave me a puzzled smile and shook her head, just once. I immediately stopped talking about Pamela.

Tatyana asked me to read something of hers, read it out loud. "To see if I got the rhythm right," she explained. I sat next to her on the sofa and read. My hand rose again and again to part the curtain of hair. It punctuated the reading. Then a hand that wasn't mine ran through my hair. "What girl wouldn't fall for you," Tatyana said. "Your hair. Your eyes. What girl can resist."

I saw it coming. She kissed me. I relived it instantly. Her shirt was unbuttoned at the top, and I saw a fine gold chain hanging from her neck. Disordered thoughts raced past me. Leaning in I saw a gold locket hanging on the chain. I leaned in some more. The contact sent me cascading. Like everything else, time began to dilate. I didn't know what to do, I couldn't see how to proceed. I had no knowledge of this territory, I had nothing, not even a map. I made myself look into her eyes, and kept looking. I didn't want to break the connection. But one of us did. A weight pulled me down and my head came to a soft landing on her thigh.

Her hand combed through my hair. I raised my head and leaned in again.

"Helmut used to call this his house," she said, pointing with her gaze to the valley between her breasts, the very top of it. It was an intriguing spot, like the tense she had used. I breathed in. I breathed it in.

Tatyana's hands were gliding over me, short landings and take-offs. She rubbed the front of my jeans like Aladdin's lamp. Somehow buttons were unbuttoned, zippers unzipped. It all seemed to lack coordination, especially me. My untutored hands kept bumping into obstacles. Neither of us was moving very fast. Time was sloshing around us. It was happening like one of those songs you've forgotten half the words of, something something something.

We lay there in the lull of late afternoon, reality at arm's length. There were things she didn't say or do. She didn't say the first time is supposed to be special. Or not supposed to be a success. She didn't suggest I wait till I had a girlfriend. She didn't make me get dressed in a hurry and shepherd me out of there.

When I saw her next, she told me a story. It was about her life, the next five years. She'd get a job. Make a good living. Sure, where she was going was a city far away where the only person she'd know would be her husband. She would have to have a child or an affair.

"How about both at the same time?" I could've said if I'd felt cheeky and self-referential.

Instead I was surprised by her act of clairvoyance. I didn't understand it and I didn't like it. I couldn't've said what would happen the following week, much less five years on. But she didn't ask me to play soothsayer. All I knew was what I felt, and not even all of that. And if she had asked, I probably would've recited one of those dead poet's lines—a line from Plath—that I'd stolen for her, one of the few that actually stayed with me, I would've said that I felt we'd boarded the train there's no getting off.

The Premonition

Aimer, c'est donner ce que l'on n'a pas à quelqu'un qui n'en veut pas—Jacques Lacan

I

The months were racing past, they were like afternoons now. Summer was back, once again the warmest yet. It was muggy, enough to make you want to shed your skin. A week had slipped by since the fire. The smell was still penetrating, it made you feel naked. They stood on the front lawn, studying the charred remains of the house.

Standing closer and peering in what had been the living-room window was the loss adjuster. This was his second visit. He was meticulous, it drove him to retrace his steps. He made his way to the back of the house, leaving Julie, Michael and Brendan where they were standing.

A burned house is an upsetting sight. But none of them seemed that perturbed, not even the owner of the house. There was in Julie's face, and in Brendan's, a strange evenness. You'd have said it was shared. Michael took it to be a kind of code, and the tightness around his mouth evidence of his efforts to break it.

Through a breach in the wall what was left of the furnace was visible. Michael followed their gaze to it.

"Do they know what caused it?" he said.

Julie shook her head. They turned to watch Brendan walk away and disappear behind the house.

"I don't think your friend likes me," Michael said.

Now it was Julie stepping away. She was fighting an impulse to agree with him. She and Michael had been together just under two years. If asked, she would've said twenty months, as if describing a toddler.

The loss adjuster was doubling back. He was scrawling in a notebook. He'd circled the house a number of times,

96

changing direction and pace. A satellite gone astray, Michael thought. Julie wondered what Brendan was doing alone in the backyard, but something in her decided not to investigate.

Michael regarded what was left of the house absently. It was old, a hundred years or more, originally a farmhouse. The field where it once stood alone had yielded to the encroaching city in a single generation. Julie had told him this and shown him photographs rescued from dusty archives. Her affection for the house weighed on him. She expressed interest in everything, architecture, history, all the other arts. She knew things, dates and events, who did what and why. It was difficult to keep up. Also, she had a passionate view of life. It set her apart.

Again, the loss adjuster disappeared behind the house. How many times had he done that? The afternoon was acquiring a certain shape, hardening into it.

"These old houses are like tinderboxes," Michael said.

That was a bookish word, tinderbox, it snagged her attention.

"You know," Julie found herself saying, "Brendan predicted it."

Michael turned to her, the unvoiced question on his lip.

"He saw it before it happened. He saw it in a dream," she said.

Which was a particularity of Julie's personality that had initially attracted him. Belief in unseen forces fed her work. It governed her soul. Michael had begun to doubt if such a thing existed, hers his anyone's. She once told him that the most striking phrase of her childhood was "second sight." She'd heard it on television. In her teens she "endowed" her late grandmother with it. It was a way of giving the notion a context, some depth, a pedigree.

Overhead, the sun blazed, asbestos-white. There was a stillness in the air, in the mood, in the weather. Earlier, neighbours had streamed through to offer sympathetic words like

97

gifts bought in the same shop. They came and went in waves of comical dismay. They all seemed to know Brendan and Julie both. Michael watched them, his thoughts circling. More than ever, he wanted to be someone else. A poet, funny and alcoholic. A captivating voice and presence. Well-attended readings, unheard-of sales figures. A success, sexually and financially. He wanted to be someone who was falling apart and had earned it. It was a view of the self that was romantic, he nursed it like a grievance. It was closing in around him. He was shedding possibilities. Six months shy of his fortieth birthday he was beginning to fear life.

"What do you mean he saw it in a dream?" he said.

Julie caught sight of Brendan returning. "I'll tell you about it later. And please don't mention it to him."

"Why not? It sounds really interesting."

"It would just upset him."

"So?"

"And it would upset me," she said. She felt her eyes narrow to slits, then widen in surprise at her reaction.

Michael took it all in. He was weighing it on some internal scale. He was a professor of comparative literature and taught at the same university where Brendan conducted his research. They had met only once before, at a party Julie had given after the first snowfall in December. The thought of it now made him tired. It was a kind of fatigue easy to equate with work. His teaching duties blunted his imagination, they sapped his desire to live a different life. He let his mind drift and recalled their most recent vacation together. They'd driven through the northeastern US. He asked Julie why half the states of New England had French names. His levity made it worse. They had fought, they continued to fight. It was like an engine running in the background. Frustration was its fuel. He thought about the ride back, which had been joyless, tense. The tarmac stretched ahead, they couldn't find exact change for the tolls, and the customs officer asked question after question with no end in sight.

Beyond sensing they were in different places in their lives, Michael and Julie avoided comparisons. It might've saved them. Julie's path seemed to open up before her, to welcome her. Michael, meanwhile, commuted daily between states of discontent.

He heard her voice and turned in her direction. He saw the grey in her eyes. He was noticing it again, seeing it new like the first time, in bed. He recalled the pure joy he felt then, that initial plunge. The circumstances now had a quality that seemed scripted, the milky light of mid-afternoon, the muffled reminders of urban life. And Julie's glow, the joy that seemed to tumble from her eyes. Grey striations surrounded her pupils like a net. That first time, that first week, was like slipping from reality.

He heard what Julie said echo back to him. The sun made him wish he'd worn a hat.

"If you want to hear something interesting, if that's what you want, ask him about his work."

But he wasn't interested. He was about to say it, too, when he noticed Brendan standing there.

"Where'd you go?" Julie asked.

"To look at the garden. It's all gone. Even the marigolds you planted."

"What marigolds?" Michael was about to ask, but Julie spoke first.

"I was just saying that interesting things have been happening at your lab."

Brendan didn't say anything to this. He seemed to be avoiding their eyes.

"How are the rats?" Michael said.

Brendan met his gaze. "Mice, actually."

"So what's going on?"

Brendan began, hesitant, almost stammering. He made adjustments as he went, pitched his voice lower, slipped significant pauses in. "The mice," he was saying, "repeated

99

behaviours acquired in earlier experiments. That was expected. What I didn't expect is that they seemed to pass this knowledge on to other mice not involved in the initial set of experiments. Some of these other mice weren't present in the lab at the time, or even born yet for that matter." Here, Brendan paused. He hadn't even looked up to gauge Michael's reaction. Instead, he looked at Julie and found the words he needed.

"As if that weren't enough, they also seemed to be showing and passing on predictive capabilities when it came to solving specific problems. Is this evidence of remote communication between mice that are, in some cases, separated by several floors? And if it is, how did they do it?"

"Cell phones?" he heard Michael say.

"Michael," Julie protested.

"Come on, are we supposed to believe this?"

Brendan forged ahead, past Michael's derision. "According to some of my colleagues, this is nothing new. They sent me back to the literature. It's been reported by many biologists. The hundredth monkey is the classic example, maybe you've heard of that. Except...."

"What?" Julie said.

"The predictive capacities. I didn't find any mention of that anywhere."

"Did you read Shaunderson finally?"

Brendan nodded.

She had suggested books by biologists who had come across similar phenomena. Books published, in some cases, 70, 80 years earlier. The most striking work was by Raynor Shaunderson, of Brasenose College, Oxford. In the nineteen-twenties, he conducted a series of experiments with simians in the zoo in Regent's Park. His findings suggested an ability on the part of the monkeys to learn as a group without any visible form of communication as long as the lessons learned possessed an "emotional charge." He published some preliminary results and for a long time wished he hadn't.

His paper appeared in an obscure journal that proved to be not sufficiently obscure. It attracted enough scorn to make his position at Oxford untenable. Shaunderson quit the college and the country.

Suddenly Brendan found the heat of the day oppressive, the smell ruinous to his health. He turned to walk away. "To see what the adjuster was up to," he claimed.

Julie looked at Michael, as if studying him.

"Tell me about his dream," he said. It was meant to stop her voicing her irritation. To salvage what was left of this day. He looked at her with expectation. Julie knew how to tell a story. She was a filmmaker, she made documentaries. Most of her time was spent planning, trying to find stories and money. Occasionally, they came together, like planets aligning. The one she was writing now was based on people who lived on her street when she was twelve. It was a cross between reminiscence and speculation. She had a working title: *The Street*. A narrow suburban avenue, leafy, comfortable. Bored Mrs. Kendall kept an eye on it from a second-floor window. She lived directly across from Julie's house— you kept swinging back into her sight line. Mrs. K. had been a nurse at one time. Now she injected life into her description of events on her street, which she reported to her husband. He seemed to be deaf in that ear. He sat watching sports on television with barely suppressed feelings of self-loathing and inadequacy. It had been twenty years since a goal or a touchdown had given him any real pleasure. With more imagination he would've craved a more destructive addiction. His wife's stories failed to rouse him. He had no interest in the games neighbours might be playing, their remedies for the murderous afternoons of suburbia, the adulterous longings played out across well-trimmed lawns.

"Tell me about it," Michael insisted, pulling at Julie's sleeve.

"After that display, I'm not sure I should."

He tugged again. "Tell me. You know you want to."

His taunt gave her pause, then propelled her forward. "Brendan called me a week ago, in the afternoon," she began, feeling her way into the narrative. "He said he'd been napping."

2

Brendan was between sleep and waking, in a passageway that was widening. Eyelid-filtered daylight got through. He woke with a start—it was cinematic. The dream was still throbbing. It was about Julie. He had seen a conflagration. It was as if its vividness made it real. Still, he kept himself from calling her, wondering if his resolve would last. He went into the bathroom—tottered was more what it felt like. He stood facing the mirror. For a moment his eyes refused to settle on his reflection. There was a dull ache behind his eyes, echoes of the dream.

The phone seemed to call to him. He dialled Julie's number. He was conscious of the length of each ring, the pause between them like a fallen bridge. Hearing her voice, Brendan let the air escape from his lungs.

"Julie, I just had the strangest dream."

"When did you start dreaming?"

More than once he had claimed not to have them. Nothing was allowed to trouble his sleep. It was one of the few things that set them apart. In life, in her work, Julie privileged dreams, their power, the weight of mystery they toted. Her own preference was for invisible forces, gaps in the web of consciousness.

"It was like a movie. The way you'd shoot it."

"Okay, now you've got my interest," she said.

"It's weird that I would experience a dream through your eyes, if you see what I mean."

"Bren, I think you should cut to the chase."

He told her that it was about her house. He saw a series

of images from the basement to the poky attic. There was a tracking shot, the camera seemed to follow pipes and ducts. Then it stopped at something like a cluster of cables. Sparks from unsheathed wiring. Then fire. An explosion and then fire. The sequence was unclear. In any event, an explosion and fire, both. Julie's house engulfed in flames.

"It was that old furnace of yours."

"That's all very charming," she said. "Did I do something lately to upset you?"

"It's just a dream. It doesn't mean anything. It makes no sense."

He insisted that it was meaningless. But it was the reason for his call. Julie had gone quiet. Lately, she'd been seeing signs everywhere, hints of the change she was certain was coming. She called it a paradigm shift—a phrase that was sure to make Brendan wince. "There's a film in it," she had scribbled in her journal. "Now is the time to make it." What was happening in Brendan's lab with the mice was part of it, and it was perfect material. Some weeks earlier she had decided to tell him. She picked him up at the laboratory where he spent so much of his time and took him to lunch at Baggio's. It was a trendy spot—teak, distressed leather, exposed brick—a semi-basement where a permanent twilight reigned. There were suits massed at the counter.

"What's happening in your experiments is really significant," she said. "More than you think. It's a sign—a shift in the way scientists view the world. Or, at least, the way you should be viewing it. I'd like to make a film about it."

His glass stopped halfway to his mouth. He produced these cinematic gestures effortlessly. His face morphed from incom- to apprehension. Julie had a sinking feeling even before he spoke; it was ghostly familiar.

"I can't talk about this stuff in a film," he said. "I'll be a laughing stock, you know that."

That was then; this was now. Speaking in measured tones into the phone, she sought to reassure him.

"You're right, you know. The dream is meaningless. It can't happen."

"What do you mean?" he asked.

"I got rid of my old furnace two months ago. I remember how much you used to worry about it."

"You never mentioned that."

"It slipped my mind."

There was something about Julie and Brendan, it wasn't part of the story she was telling, it wasn't for Michael's consumption. Her connection with Brendan was unusual. They had known each other a long time. They were friends. Close, but only. Still, they'd imagined how it might be. It never really surfaced in conversation. If it had, they would've been able to measure the discrepancies. Raised on storytelling, Julie possessed an unfair advantage. She'd seen boundless afternoons together, subtle rifts in time. A room somewhere. The sound of the ocean below the shuttered window, too distant to seem real. Their lives quietly moved ahead, years on which the stars set without a murmur. Their lives followed a pattern, converging and diverging. Converging. Invisibly they spun the thread.

"You had your furnace replaced?"

"I did." She found herself driven to explain this in meticulous detail, the day it happened, the name of the contractor, his tousled hair and fortyish boyishness.

"I'm glad, Julie."

Silence followed silence.

"Okay," he said.

"Okay."

"Are you going?"

"Is there something you...?" she said.

"No, I'm all right. I'll speak to you soon."

3

Imagine an establishing shot. Julie's house, intact. She lived alone, she always had. There were years when she made money and years when it was scarce. In one of the leanest she bought a house—this house. Unhurriedly she furnished it, items from all over, things she hadn't particularly looked for. Her life was her own, it was a work in progress.

The doorbell rang. Framed in the doorway was Brendan. Not ten minutes earlier he'd been on the phone.

"How'd you get here so fast?"

"I took a cab."

"A cab?" she said, incredulous.

"Aren't you going to ask me in?"

She dance-stepped to one side and welcomed him with a flourish. "You remember the way to the basement."

"Julie," he said, not really protesting.

"Take a look, you'll feel better."

"I just had a sudden urge to see you. It's been so long."

"Go see the furnace first."

They both smiled. It released him. He bounded down the stairs and, after a moment, ran back up. He praised the look of the new furnace, it had a sheen of efficiency, it was a fine piece of machinery, explosion-proof. The verbal riff made Julie smile.

"It's not like you to heed dreams."

Brendan shrugged. Julie levelled a look at him, bemused, almost appraising. He gave her a quizzical smile—there was mischief in it, too. Her lower lip dropped slightly, and held. The moment was meant to be savoured. Or seized. He was seeing her for the first time in weeks. It was like an unexpected encounter in a crowd. There she was, the cropped hair, which was new, her eyes, the slivers of grey like needles. Something about her. The translucence of her skin, of her expressions. He watched her, he became aware of it. He stood there unable to make a move.

She was different from everyone he knew. Even as long ago as grade school she stood apart. Julie grew up against a backdrop of Greek mythology. Legendary books filled the house, Homer, Virgil, Euripides. Her mother had studied the Classics. Along with her daughter, the ancient world was her passion. She enlisted Julie through bedtime stories. The gods and demi-gods tumbled from a young girl's dreams, they occupied the house like benevolent ghosts.

She offered him Scotch. It was mid-afternoon, they'd forgotten the time. She found no Scotch in the cabinet, only Michael's blended Irish whiskey. Still, Brendan accepted the drink and even toasted Michael's health. He thought she might ask about the lab. What was happening in his experiments she continued to find fascinating. She thought of Shaunderson, and so did he. In 1929, he left England and controversy behind. So began his years in the wilderness, literally. In the woods of Borneo he continued to conduct his research with primates. This was the work that established his brief notoriety. During that period, the last five years of his life, he was wracked by symptoms of a nervous condition brought on by the humiliation he had suffered in England.

Brendan had read Shaunderson's books, and one slim biography, more than once. It was the closest he would come to Shaunderson's missionary zeal. Although Julie had once called science his mistress, Brendan didn't really choose science. A high-school counsellor had talked him into Biology and no-one had come around to talk him out of it. In Julie's view his contribution to science was important. Occasionally, she rained encouragement on him. There were times when his work began to seem huge. He had ability, that was clear, and the mysteries of biology secretly pleased him.

Julie sipped her whiskey and didn't ask about his work. She didn't want to discuss his dream, either, but found she couldn't dismiss it—a state she recognized as an impediment to conversation. Having drunk Michael's health,

Brendan now asked how he was.

"He's teaching a couple of courses."

Which sounded to Brendan like no answer at all. What did he care? She could have told him that Michael wanted to write a novel, and the time to do it. His love of literature had trapped him in a pattern of consumption. For years he devoured books and hardly wrote a line. His already modest output had fallen off. Now he had the merest outlines of a novel like something glimpsed in a dream. He was devoting two or three hours a week to it, that was it. He had looked forward to a summer free of teaching to make headway. Then, inexplicably, he agreed to teach two summer courses. He was conscious of wasting precious days. Looking ahead, all he saw was more preparation and lecturing. More grading. A new school year in September. Precious months, squandered.

Asking about Michael was a mistake, Brendan saw that now. The effect on Julie's mood was unmistakable. She politely offered him another drink, which he no less politely declined. She offered to drive him back, and he accepted.

4

"Don't tell me," Michael said. "You drove him back just in time to see that it was his house that had burned down to the ground."

"Not quite to the ground, as you can see," Julie said.

He tried to keep the emotion he felt from disfiguring him. Her story was like a blow, it left his body feeling misaligned. Something was happening. Or had already happened. He reached in a pocket for his cigarettes—he'd taken it up again—and pulled one out of its foil coffin. He offered her one in answer to her disapproving look.

Julie's story triggered another physical reaction. There was an unpleasant secretion in his throat. He wanted to spit out an objection but something—the futility of it—kept him from it. A sort of understanding between them was taking shape.

"Why didn't you mention this before?" he managed to say.

"Brendan asked me not to."

"What does that mean?"

There was a delay in her response. "I guess it spooked him."

"No, I don't mean that," he said.

Brendan was coming back, preceded by his shadow on the lawn. Julie and Michael looked up. In the distance, the adjuster was walking to his car.

"Is he leaving?" Julie said. "What did he say?"

"He said he was sorry for my loss."

JASMINA ODOR

In Vancouver, with David

I remember well this lunch I had one day with David's, my boyfriend David's, Aunt Joyce. I had gone to her apartment, for the first time, to pick up some tickets she had promised the two of us. She worked at a small theatre that put on satires, black comedies and such. I think she was a sort of secretary there. So I came for the tickets, and she said somebody was just about to bring them by—they were late, in fact, she said—and so she invited me in for lunch. "It'll give us a chance to visit, love," she said, in her pleasant voice that *carried*, like everyone's voice should, if they plan to be generally successful in life. She rubbed my shoulder with one hand and motioned me in with the other. She was very heavy, with a familiar kind of pretty, friendly face. I sat down at a little table separated from the kitchen by a counter. I liked that she called me "love," and in general I liked women, older women, calling me by terms of endearment. Joyce wore big tunics and ornamental earrings with stones that matched the colours of her outfits and the colour of her polished fingernails.

As I sat, her dog Milka, of a breed I would not have known myself if Joyce hadn't told me that she's a Field Spaniel, occasionally came to sniff and rub up against me. Milka got her name from the German chocolate, Joyce said as she set the table and brought out garlic mashed potatoes, a pan of veggie-sausages, and one of those store-bought potato salads. Then she called for the dog, who had disappeared a moment ago, saying "Come here girl," over and over, she must have said it eight or nine times, with the same intonation each time. Milka eventually bounced along and climbed onto a chair beside me. "You don't mind if Milky eats with us," Joyce said, said and not really asked, as she set a soup bowl in front of the dog. I didn't know what to say. The dog put its paws beside the bowl. It raised itself up and leaned in to smell the sausage, tongue hanging out. Joyce motioned it to sit back down and began cutting a sausage for it into small pieces. I still didn't know what to do, or where to look. Then I caught the smell of the dog's breath, and with that the obscenity of the situation, of eating at a table with a dog, struck me. And I began to feel shamefully uneasy, like I was involved in something perverse. My parents, whom David sometimes—inaccurately, I think—called "properly European," came to mind, and I felt even more ashamed on their behalf. What ridiculousness, I remember thinking. Then, as if scripted, the man with the tickets came. I remember that he leaned in through the door, extended his arm in a wave and called out "Hi, Milka girl, well look at you," in a baby voice. When he left, Joyce sat down and spooned some sausage and potato stuff onto my plate. I ate it, the dog ate hers, Joyce prattled on. Finally I excused myself and left the whole nauseating circus.

When I met with David that night—at a little café on Edmonton's trendiest avenue, a café with a clientele, I remember thinking disdainfully as I approached it that evening, that considered itself *artistic* and *radical*—I broke up with him. I saw him through the glass front, sitting at a table by the wall, bent over a magazine and, in a characteristic gesture, stroking his jaw. I walked up to him, laid the tickets on the table. I said, "Here are the tickets, you'll have to find someone to go with, 'cause I'm not going with you, I'm not going anywhere with you again." David said, "What the fuck are you talking about?" But I just walked right out, with all my anger tight inside me. We got back together, so to speak, the next day. David had a way with me, I should admit. He called me on the phone in the morning, five or six times before I actually answered. The first thing he said to me was "Lidi," in that soft, sort of vulnerable, voice, and I knew then that we weren't, of course, over.

That was in May, the episode that David later called my mini-breakdown. We had been dating for a year then, I worked in a bookstore, and David was a bartender. My hours were long and leisurely and occasionally contemplative, and David's hours were charged and tense and exhausting. David also thought himself something of a poet and wrote poems with words like *lacunae* and *orbits*, poems I didn't understand. I looked for pieces of prettiness, tongues pressed to petals, stuff like that, in his poems, and for any oblique mention of me. But he wasn't pretentious, David. My parents liked him well enough, although he wasn't the Croatian boyfriend they had hoped for, just a Canadian, Anglican boy whose background had nothing in common with mine, with *our* background as my parents would say. He'll never understand that, they'd say.

In June of that same year a cousin of mine who lived in Vancouver, who was older than I and married with children, invited me for a visit and said I should bring David. "I love the West Coast, Vancouver is great," David said, "We should go." West Coast, East Coast, out west, up north, these are the ways Canadians orientate themselves around their country, I thought, such a humongous country and all there is to it is left, right, up, down. So we went to Vancouver, drove the twelve or so hours in David's blue Pontiac Sunbird. We were getting relatively close, we were well past Kamloops when the sun was setting, so we were driving into the sunset. "Write that, David," I said, "write that we are driving into the sunset, that your hand is inside my clothes, that we are the only survivors of an apocalypse." David often smiled with just one side of his mouth. "I would," he said, "but I don't have a free hand. You write it."

My cousin Zrinka and her husband Marco lived in a white-and-yellow, two-storey house in the Grandview area, next to a corner store. Their daughters were six and eight years old. One was named Lidija, like me, except they spelled it Lydia, the English way, and the other Antonia, nice universal names, my cousin said. Zrinka talked to them in Croatian, Marco in Italian, and the girls answered in

English. Their house had an official guest-room, and David and I slept on the futon in it. Zrinka had lived in Vancouver for twelve years, twice as long as I'd been in Edmonton. Marco had lived there since he was five years old, and I wondered sometimes, listening to him repeat simple instructions in Italian to one of the girls, how much of the language he had lost. It was my first time meeting him; he was pale, with dark hair that must have only recently begun to recede, and seemed to wear flip-flops and Adidas shorts everywhere. At breakfast, the morning after we arrived—it was Saturday—Marco asked me what I'm planning to do, now that I'm "finished school and everything." "Your degree's in history, right?" he said. People always ask what you're planning to do, this ridiculous question, and everyone, I've always thought, lies, says they're looking into things, mentions a school or a company they've only heard about in conversation, say they're taking a year off to travel. Who considers that there may be a natural disaster, or something of the sort, that decides for them. Falling in love, I thought, is a natural disaster, and once I thought it, it seemed like quite a clever comparison. "Zrinka said you were thinking of going down home for a while," he continued. Their kitchen was small and neat and entirely white. "What's with you and the questions? They're here on vacation," Zrinka said, and took away his plate with half a slice of bacon still on it, and so breakfast was over.

David and I meant to go to the University of British Columbia campus during the day, but it was already dusk when we got there. Part of the delay was an argument between him and me about his socks, which we had had before. "Dress pants and loafers and white socks?" I noticed them just as he was opening the screen-door to let us out of the house. "Aw fuck," he said, and rolled his eyes. "I'm gonna wear pink socks and sandals one day, just to piss you off." While I went off upstairs to the guest-room, to look for socks in our as yet unpacked suitcase, he went to the kitchen to open a beer. When I returned downstairs, he got me a cranberry cooler, and socks in hand we sat in the living-room and watched a talk show. Some two hours later we finally got in the car and drove to the campus. After parking the car, we walked and walked, with no clear goal, until we got down to this pavilion that had a view of the sea, and stone arches, green bushes, a fountain in the centre. At the edge of it was a stone fence from which you looked down on a road and some lawn a few metres below, and further beyond that you saw the sea stretching out, it was a dense blue that night. Zrinka was right in saying it isn't really like the Adriatic, where we had both spent many summers, and a few of them together, at her parents' summer house. But that was when I was still a kid, when I watched Zrinka enviably as she went out every night (bare-shouldered, skin smelling of coconut suntan lotion), when neither of us could have imagined we would meet here, of all places, one day. David and I leaned our torsos on the low wall and hung our arms over the edge. "Hot skin against cool stone," David recited in a mock voice. The stone was actually warm and suddenly it all seemed strange, this perfectly neat, fake little pavilion behind us and the ocean distant and inconceivable. "Let's go," I said, turning away from the view. David looked at me, looked back, and stayed as he was. "I'll meet you in the car," he said.

We were all meant to go out for drinks that night, but at the last minute Zrinka said she would stay home with the kids, and so it was the three of us, David, Marco and I, who got into Marco's secondhand Volkswagen, and headed downtown. We scored a seat on a patio of a café whose name I don't remember, it was on Robson Street, or off Robson Street, either way. We smoked cigarettes, drank gin and tonics. The patio was raised three steps from the sidewalk and surrounded by a low railing, next to which we sat, and watched the crowds that poured by on the street, the night warm and lovely in a way I couldn't remember it ever being

in Edmonton. At some point Marco started talking to someone at the table next to ours. I didn't pay attention because
I didn't want to become part of the conversation. David
seemed to be in the same mood as me, and just sat looking.
We were joined by our forefingers, our arms over the railing.
Marco spoiled it when he began introductions with the man
at the next table, who wore a suit jacket, was in his thirties,
apparently drinking alone. On his table sat a cell phone, a
cigarette case and something like an electronic day-planner,
or palm pilot maybe. He promptly offered his Marlboros
around. I still tried to look disinterested, smiling faintly and
staring off vacantly. The crowds were engrossing to me,
never-ending variations. Street people passed often, but few
stopped beside us, we were part of the background to them.
A round of drinks arrived, courtesy of the man David and I
were trying to ignore. I toasted with everyone and turned
back around. Then a street guy walking slowly along the
sidewalk made eye contact with me; he had a greying beard
and a canvas bag, which had the word Vancouver splashed
on it in several colours, slung on his shoulder. He walked
over and, without touching the railing he said, "Can you
spare, ma'am, I haven't eaten, ma'am, a dollar or a quarter."
As I was reaching for my purse the yuppie said, "Hey why
don't you come over here, I've got more money for you." He
pulled out a $5 bill. "Five bucks if you'll suck my cock," said
this yuppie, elbowing Marco to laugh with him. The man,
the man with the canvas bag, he frowned, and muttered
something indistinct but vaguely angry-sounding, and then
walked away.

Back at Zrinka's house, David and I lay on the bed in the
guest-room with the lights turned off and the window open,
still in our clothes. My back was turned to him and he held
me because I was crying, sobbing and crying, I don't know
how long before he calmed me down. He turned me around
to face him and then held me like that, my face in his chest,

so that it seemed I cried into him, he absorbed it all. I was not sure why I was crying, because of that stupid man, or maybe the ocean, or David himself, certainly I didn't like to be crying for no clear reason. At the café I had tried to throw a drink at that guy, but I'd done it so awkwardly that most of the scotch, which he had ordered us a moment earlier, landed on the floor, only some on the guy's knee, and a fair bit on Marco. Ridiculous it all felt; even leaving—shaking as I was for some reason—could not be done right because so many people, unintentionally I'm sure, blocked the way. David's hand found me just as I started down the sidewalk, then Marco caught up with us, looking embarrassed, I don't know for whom, and we drove home in silence. In the guest-room then David held me so tight that I had to laugh a little and say, "I can't breathe, David," and he said "You don't have to breathe air, you can just breathe me," and then he started reciting lines, nonsense lines, "Beneath the surface of the ocean we'll be joined, your hair will be a nest for my lips—do you hear, or have you suffocated?" "I've suffocated," I said, mostly into his chest. He continued, until, with a word still half in his mouth, he fell asleep. I knew the precise moment because I felt his limbs go heavy and, within seconds, his breathing became regular. I wanted to stay awake, to feel him sleep like that, but the next thing I remember is the opening and closing of doors, feet on the stairs, dishes clinking, and outside, the purring sound of cars softly turning corners.

Peanuts

This morning the satellite guy is at our house. The guy is young, tall, modestly good looking. After I lead him into the living-room, my daughter Amanda brings him in a Coke. I see him do a double take at her, and then steal another glance as she walks away. This isn't out of the ordinary, of course—my daughter is an unusual beauty. I kind of wished she would give him a second glance, or sit in the living-room and chat with him. I could picture her rather well with a guy like this. But she's not terribly talkative with strangers.

Now, people say Amanda looks like me. She does in a way, but there's a difference between nice looking and gorgeous, although it's hard to say where precisely that difference lies. Amanda looks a little bit like me and a little bit like my sister Grace, and yet Grace is quite plain, I'm pretty, and Amanda is stunning. If you catch sight of her in half-profile, there is something extraordinary about the angle of her jaw and the elongated cheek. Her grey eyes aren't big, but they're wide, and above them sit two perfectly straight, long eyebrows. If you looked at it simply mathematically, you might say her face is too long, but I think most real beauties have something seemingly incongruous about their faces. The resemblance between us reminds me of a picture I saw once, of a supermodel and her three sisters, just an impromptu photo, and in it all the women looked quite a bit alike, had the same straight noses and the same wide eyes, and yet only one was beautiful.

Just as the satellite guy is packing up in the living-room, Amanda does in fact walk in and give him a big wide smile. It is this spontaneous, modest smile that she's had since childhood, which often, like today, makes me well up with affection for her. And just as the guy leaves, my husband arrives from work. He's carrying files under his arm, and his step is light but a little tired. Dan still looks youthful, but sometimes I think he's getting some old-man habits. Every day when he gets home from work, he goes upstairs briefly, washes up but doesn't change, just takes off his watch, his tie, changes his socks, and comes back down and pours a little glass full of whisky. He then sits in the middle of the sofa with his feet up on the stool, sighs a little bit, and this serene half-smile hangs about his lips.

Dan has also started cooking and collecting recipes from the *Canadian Living* magazine. He watches—well, we watch—travel shows and cooking shows, and we make note of not only recipes, but drink mixes, and all-natural skin treatments, and detoxifying vegetable juices. Today Dan kisses me fully on the lips and smells my hair, and I pat his hip. Once he's settled in on the sofa, I bring my coffee with me, curl up next to him, and he calls me love and asks what I did today. He calls Amanda over too, and she sits on the other side of him, and they proceed to talk sweet nonsense to each other, rub noses, squeeze each other's kneecaps. He then turns to me with a look that seems not only serene but wistful. In a few minutes Amanda gets up to begin the elaborate process of getting ready for a night out. The same process that will leave the bathroom moist and fragrant, and the doorknobs greasy with lotion. And Amanda too will become moist and fragrant, and flushed and sparkling. It can be my favourite part of the night, to see her bounce down the stairs, all made up like that, and then bounce back up because she's forgotten something, and then down again, and so on. Regularly Dan and I forget whatever it is we're watching on television and just marvel at our own daughter.

I have to say, however, that the guys she dates are hardly as interesting as you might imagine a girl like her dating. And she seems to date casually, a few months with this boy, a few weeks with another. Without fail they are polite little men, and very stylish either in a teenage kind of way, or in an imitation of the young professionals. Most of them have highlights in their hair, blond or honey brown; they wear well-tailored suit jackets and square-toed shoes. Inevitably, as I open the door, there is the young man saying, "Good evening, Mrs. Reikson," and leaning in to shake my hand. They are all like that, eager to make a good impression. Often they bring a bottle of wine, and often they try to make amusing comments about the traffic, or the weather, or about the design of our house, which is architecturally speaking a marvel, even among the other well-built houses on our block.

Tonight, though, it's Amanda's girlfriend Talia ringing the door bell. Amanda emerges from the kitchen, a big yellow pear stuck in her mouth as she's using both hands to button up her jacket. She waves goodbye, they leave, and Dan and I go upstairs before coming back down to watch television.

I read somewhere that people don't age gradually, but in spans of about seven years. Every seven years or so all our cells replace themselves. Apart from that, it seems amazing to me that a person goes from infancy to old age, yet every day wakes up looking the same. Every morning you see the same person in the mirror, yet suddenly that person is middle-aged, or old. No wonder it takes us by surprise. But I also think there must be a point in everyone's life when they first realize they are ageing. When I was about 22 or 23, Grace and I were on vacation on the west coast. We were trying on bathing-suits, and I remember looking at her body— a body I knew well—and seeing that it would pass into a different stage. She was a splendidly built girl, tall and long-legged, with these small, fragile shoulders, little breasts, a long neck and thin arms. She was all like that, slim and long, but not sharp or muscular anywhere, just round and elongated. But that time I could see how her tummy would eventually round out, her breasts come to look even smaller, how her thighs would get heavy, and she would become something else. And as I saw her body pass into another stage, so I saw, of course, my own body as one in transition.

Dan cuddles with me until about midnight. I stay up watching a travel show on the Outdoor Network. I'm wearing my embroidered-silk robe, my favourite, and thick thermal socks, and I'm inexpressibly comfortable. I've finished a glass of steamed milk, and I think I feel myself finally drifting toward sleep. The clock is showing ten after two in the morning. The narrating traveller on the TV is now in Nepal, attending a wedding of one bride to four brothers. Does this really happen, I wonder, and then I don't care anymore. I turn off the television. As I shut off the light, I hear a car outside, and I peek through the half-open curtain to see the car stop on the sidewalk and Amanda get out of the passenger seat. As I'm walking to the kitchen it occurs to me that Talia's car is a different model. Amanda walks in and is surprised to see me—I'm hardly ever up when she gets home. I ask drowsily how her night was. She looks a little drowsy herself. Her eyes have lost all their makeup and her lids are sitting low. Her cheeks are a little puffy, like after a nap. On a second look I realize she is even missing an earring. For a moment I'm struck by the splendidness of this sight, my daughter looking tired, dishevelled and caught off guard. I feel like hugging her momentarily. But I don't want to ambush her. Instead, on an impulse, I ask, "Who was that who dropped you off?" I instantly regret asking and prolonging her discomfort. It's clear she just wants to go upstairs.

"Huh? We ran into some people from school, that's all."

Amanda isn't prone to lying by any stretch, and when she does it she looks positively embarrassed. She gets a little frown between her eyebrows. I wish her goodnight and walk up the stairs without looking back at her.

The next Friday Dan comes home from work late.

"There's just a bit of trouble at work again," he says. He beats the armrest with an open palm while mouthing the words again: "a bit of trouble." Dan is an executive assistant at a public relations firm. It's a small company, as far as their type goes, but quite successful. Dan's been with them for fourteen years now. Every so often he comes home with "a bit of trouble." He tells me, rather disconnectedly, about a questionable contract, a minor one, and a client concerned over conflict of interest—"So?" I ask.

"So nothing," he says.

I make him take off his tie, and fix him a drink, since he refuses to eat. We watch television.

"Millie," he says after a while, "this place needs dusting." He swipes a finger alongside the leg of the coffee table. Little things irritate Dan when he's got a bigger problem on his mind.

By the end of next week, Dan tells me they've ordered an independent investigation into the bungled account. This hasn't happened to him before, as far as I know. When Amanda comes home from her dance lesson—her dark hair all windblown, her cheeks pink, stunning even in her white windbreaker—we sit in the living-room, the three of us, the TV is on but the sound low, and actually we all drink, even Amanda, and we talk sporadically, sometimes small talk, sometimes about Dan's situation. Dan drinks bourbon, and the two of us gin with cranberry juice; the small assortment of bottles sits on the table, and we keep refilling as we please. We don't even have supper, except for the mixed nuts that always sit on the table, and some crackers with cream cheese that Amanda brings in at some point. Finally, around ten o'clock—I don't even know where the time's gone—we all get thirsty, and after going to the kitchen for water Dan decides he'll go up to bed. He pulls on my earlobes, kisses me. I say I'll be right up.

The next day the article comes out in the "Announcer," a long column on the second-last page of the business section. "Controversy at Beiland Inc," the title reads. And underneath it in italics, *Several middle-level executives may face sus-*

pension. Dan's name is not on that list, but it is mentioned, followed by "implicated."

"It was bound to be written about," I say as we're sitting across from each other that afternoon. He's staring into space rather intently.

"Of course," he says, with a little frown, as if annoyed that I've interrupted a reverie. "But I wouldn't have thought it—" he looks up at me wistfully, then looks around the kitchen, pauses at each corner, as if it weren't in fact his own kitchen.

"If I could go back in time," he says, and he laughs, the laughter issuing from behind his hands as they cover his face. I get him to put his head in my lap. He pretends to resist, and we have a mock tug-of-war. I call him my boy, my skinny boy, too skinny to marry, like my mother used to say, I call him my love and my life sentence. Amanda comes home from school and she looks to be in a dark mood too. For a moment I remember her coming home that night last week, and I wonder if I should be worried about anything. But I let it go.

The weekend passes slowly. We don't do anything. The tickets we had for the ballet on Saturday we give away at the last minute. Dan says he has no patience for sitting still for two and a half hours. The phone seems to be ringing constantly, until we just shut off the ringer. There are messages that I don't care to listen to. One is from Grace; 'Millie— and Dan, I was hoping to' she begins, but I cut it off without listening to the rest. On Sunday, neither Dan nor I leave the house. We don't get dressed, and we listen to old records. We dance a little bit, around the coffee table, getting tangled in our housecoats. We drink. By the time night falls we are drunk and impenetrable.

On Monday, Amanda is home early from school. I'm cooking some frittatas and thinking about the ballet on Saturday. I can't believe we gave the tickets away to the Van Tiers from across the street. The same people who call us only immediately before and after asking for a favour. The same Beatrice Van Tier who called me this morning—two days later—to say they loved it, what a stunning performance, and then she cut me off with, "Sorry I can't chat, dear, I got some people on the way." I wish now that I had ripped the tickets into little pieces and swallowed them, rather than given them to that bitch. But I hadn't, so here we are now. Amanda sits down on the stool at the breakfast nook and picks at the corners of my frittatas. She thinks we should go do something, she and I, get out of the house for a bit, do some shopping. My car is in the shop, but she says we can take the bus. I look outside through the window.

"It's warm out," Amanda says. "Just a little muggy."

But it's not the weather I'm evaluating, not quite. I would prefer to be home when Dan gets home from work. We leave him a message on his voice mail. "Amanda and I are setting sail to this ship. Remember us with love. Or call my cell if you need us." We walk a block to the bus stop; Amanda wants to go to the thrift store.

"Are you actually going to buy anything here?" I ask her as the bus lurches to a stop.

"I always do," she says, though that's news to me. Inside, the store is bustling, which is explained by the big cardboard signs that say 50% off. We move in the narrow space between the overstuffed rows of clothing. I think about last night; Dan wanted to talk in bed for a long time. We ate a huge supper of veal, late, and I think it kept us up. What Dan wanted to talk about, mostly, was stuff from the past. About the time when I worked as a waitress in a little diner, how he would sit around until closing time, and then count my cash while I cleaned the kitchen.

The whole time as Amanda and I move from section to section, women's clothing, men's clothing, housewares, there is a very fat young woman in front of us, with small feet in thin cotton runners, wearing tights, and wheeling a big cart. She coos to her little child, whose little socked feet are hanging from the child seat in the cart. After we have been here almost an hour, I can't stand to look at her anymore, nor at the rows of old shoes, they are too pathetic. But then I see the toy section, and think that perhaps the saddest things are the little bags of goodies, old cloth dolls, and Barbies, and colouring books, maybe a Rubik's cube, stuffed inside clear plastic bags stapled shut.

"We should go," I say to Amanda, "it's going to rain."

Through the store windows I can see the overcast sky. We get into a line-up—they're all easily twenty people long. Finally, at the till, the man wearing the orange store vest smiles widely at Amanda.

"Hello, stranger," he says. She says hello back, then turns to me.

"Oh, Mom, this is Earl," and to him, "this is my mom."

I shake Earl's extended hand. He says "Good to meet you." He greets me as if it's the commonest thing for him to be introduced to customers while working his cash in the middle of a sale rush.

"Found some nice things, did you," he says as he folds the shirts into a plastic bag. He smiles at me as I hand him money. As we're walking away, Amanda says, "I'll see you." I can't help but throw a second glance at Earl, which only confirms what I already caught of him—a shortish figure in his late twenties, a round face framed by short black hair and a short beard. Outside it's steadily drizzling.

"A friend of yours?" I say.

"Yeah," she says.

It's only when we get off the bus and are walking toward the house in darkness, that Amanda stops. We're both wet by now; I can see our house a little further down, and the lights are on inside it. Amanda has put her hood on, she is sniffling, and there are smudges around her eyes.

"The thing is," she says, "the thing is, Mum, I think I'm in love." She rubs her nose a little.

"With Earl," she then says, and with her thumb points to

the direction we've just come from. I half expect this Earl to materialize in the light of the streetlamp and stand waiting for my response. Instead there's just the sound of rain, a car driving down the next block, and my fallen-in-love daughter standing at the edge of a puddle. Of course, I think. It seems perfectly clear, and yet I don't understand it.

"Mom?" she says.

"Who *is* Earl?" I say. She looks confused. Confused and somehow annoyingly apprehensive.

"I mean, who is he? Is he your boyfriend? Where did you find him?"

Her face changes, closes up. "I met him at a friend's house. He's 32. Years old. But I love him."

Well then. "And for how long have you loved this Earl?" I ask her.

"Kind of a long time now. Almost five months."

I don't know what else to say. I take her hand and lead her, in a sense, toward the house. I want to say something else, perhaps something nice, but I don't have it in me.

Inside the house, I leave her in the hallway and call out to Dan. The lights are on in the kitchen and living-room, but he's not in either. I proceed upstairs. In the bedroom, he is on his knees in front of the walk-in closet. He is rummaging through the contents of some boxes; there are papers, stacks of them, and also unopened photo albums, sweaters, and computer disks, strewn all around him. I also spot the familiar glint of the purple-glass key chain attached to the safe key, though the room divider in front of the actual safe seems untouched. To my left, on our thick, ecru-coloured, imported rug, is a large stain, its edges peeking out from underneath more sheets of paper. The duvet is crumpled on the floor beside the bed.

"What are you doing?" I say when he looks up at me.

"What? I'm looking for something. The miracle that will prove me innocent. And the thing—don't step in that, babe, I spilled some whisky." All the while he is eyeing the things around him and moving them slightly.

"You know what really chokes me, Millie, in the end? That it's just peanuts, you know, I mean, all this, for what—peanuts."

"All which?" I say. When he was much younger, Dan used to sit like he's doing now, kneeling with his legs spread open.

He leans forward then, so far that he digs his forehead into the carpet. His hands are still at his side.

"And how was your day, dear?" he asks then, from his hole in the sand.

"It was fine," I say, and I bring myself down to sit on my haunches too.

"A strange night, maybe. Dan—" I extend my hand and lean in his direction.

"Where's Amanda?" he asks.

Amanda is in a world in which five months is a long time, I want to say. Amanda is in love. But I don't say either just then.

"She's here," I say instead, just as I start to crawl toward Dan. And indeed, we both look up then to see her standing in the doorway.

You Can't Stay Here

Ivona works as a cleaning woman; she vacuums a restaurant, after 2 AM, when everyone has gone home. The restaurant is called "Comfort Food Den," and it is on the ground floor of a three-storey pink-stucco structure, below a set of law offices. Though all the staff has left by the time she arrives, she sees traces of them in many places: notes posted by the front till—*groups reserving for eight or more must be told about 15% gratuity*—written in a bubbly cursive, or in the bar section an ashtray with two butts in it tucked away beside the sink, last indulgences of the night while closing, perhaps. Although she doesn't clean the kitchen, she wanders in there occasionally, on nights that feel long and expansive; sometimes she slides open the clear-glass door of the dessert cooler to cut herself a slice of pie that she then eats with her fingers. And she has taken to eating pie—apple, or lemon meringue—while standing in front of the staff table in the corner and reading notices posted above it. Messages on white letter paper in purple marker: *"All staff: The days-off book is getting ridiculous. I'm trying to run a business here!"* Signed *"Will."* Every few weeks a new message pops up and sometimes a whole bunch, giving the impression of a crisis; their tones are threatening, exasperated, sarcastic. *"All staff: our closing time is 10 PM. Which means we serve customers until 10 PM. If anyone has issues with this please see me personally. Will."* One of her favourites is *"Staff: eating gummy worms while on shift (or off!) constitutes stealing."*

She has been cleaning the restaurant for about six months when she sees the notice (on the board that stands on the front lawn), seeking, immediately, a daytime hostess. The idea of being present in the same space, but during the day, when everything happens, tempts her. The only barrier is uncertainty about her English skills, her ability to pronounce menu items clearly, not to mix up round *o*s and flat *o*s, to deliver the daily special smoothly, without the awkwardness of misunderstanding. But she feels it is a necessary step now, and imagines her accent will at least bring a dissonant note to this comfy, middle-class family operation.

She knows enough to apply after 2 PM, when the restaurant is nearly empty. The girl at the front is young and pleasant and uninterested. She takes Ivona's resumé, typed up the night before on a neighbour's computer, and hands her an application form, a crooked photocopy asking for employment history and personal interests in crowded block lettering. Ivona is working through it in a booth near the door, when a man wearing a tie emerges from the kitchen. As he sits down opposite her, and shakes her hand—"I'm Will"—his smile seems calm, and real. He looks young to her, barely in his thirties. He is neither middle-aged, nor pompous, as she's imagined. He is of average height, and slim and pleasant-looking and chatty. He mentions his teenage daughter, who apparently has the same curly hair Ivona does. He tells her he is actually 43, after she comments that he looks too young to have a teenage daughter. "It's been a kind of a crazy house here," he says, "so don't mind me if I seem a bit cranky." He asks where her accent is from. She tells him it's Croatian, and he replies that his parents are Belgian. "I'll be calling you by tomorrow, I think," he says. "Everything looks good. I'm pretty sure everything will be good."

Ivona and Sven had got engaged nine years ago, when they were still living in Croatia. His parents disliked her, for intangible reasons, but nonetheless sharply for it. "She is a little, well, a little hoity," Sven's mother said, after Ivona visited the house for the first time, and to accompany her comment she did a strut from the stove to the table, with her nose held high and her hips jerking from side to side. They tolerated her well enough perhaps, in that way that parents sometimes have with their children, affectionate but beneath it a little spiteful and a little hateful. "I don't understand what they want out of me," Ivona would say to Sven. He in turn soothed her, said they were just a little over-possessive of their only son, and besides, she's not marrying *them*. She agreed, generally; she never doubted that he was worth it.

In honour of Ivona's and Sven's engagement, his parents held, at their house, a gathering, a supper where some twenty guests ate in shifts of eight, as many as the dining-room table could accommodate. Ivona wore a dress she had had made just a few weeks earlier, a present to herself. She was feeling lavish and loved and eager in those days. While the second round of guests were eating, she walked around the table, adding dishes, taking away plates, nudging children to eat. Sven's father sat at the head, having grown impatient and not wanting to wait for the last round. He was bald, sarcastic and funny. As Ivona was taking the full bone-plate beside him, to replace it with a new one, he said casually, looking at her sideways, "I see you're looking stylish. What are those, flowers, on your dress? Roses are in bloom for you guys, I guess." People looked over to smile. She put a clean plate on the table. "But maybe it should be a little longer, your dress"—he looked down—"to cover your calves. You have calves," he continued, "like a Frenchman who spent his life stepping on grapes in a barrel." It was moments like these that still stood starkly in Ivona's mind, part of the landscape of her marriage.

Will starts flirting with Ivona after a few weeks of hiring her as his daytime hostess. She notices he flirts with all the weekend girls (she works a few weekends), most of whom are in school or filling time after finishing school. He pulls lightly on their ponytails and leans in to smell their necks. He gets a little frantic when asked for days off, but usually gives in. "You are such a lady, you know, Ivona," he says to her almost every day now. "How is your husband, is he treating you right?" he says, often too. "Because if he isn't, you shouldn't take that." She has heard it before and found it curious, this turn of phrase, association of love with being "treated right." It makes her think of pets, or livestock, something helpless. Dogs should be treated right—not kept inside too much, fed regularly, petted a lot. Will's wife Kim comes to the restaurant only occasionally. She has shoulder-length hair dyed blond, and curled into large, girlish locks. When she is at the restaurant, she spends most of the day assessing the staff's habits, the clutter on the counter, the cleanliness of the glasses, and Will stays mostly in his office at the back of the bar.

One day, as Ivona is giving Will her daily cash-out, he motions her into the office. He asks how her day was. While looking at him she has a brief thought that he has been crying, there is moistness in the corners of his eyes. "I had a dream about you," he says, after some small talk. "Oh, this is embarrassing," he says, "I shouldn't say this, it's really bad, but you were naked in it."

Ivona and her husband Sven have a six-year-old son, Mario. Mario is autistic and without any special talents (unlike some children featured in brochures and magazines on autism, gifted painters, etc.). He is, however, a beautiful child, with smooth, shiny brown hair and flushed cheeks. Perhaps for this reason, strangers generally expect him to be exceptionally responsive, and affectionate, and bright, but he isn't any of these things. On one occasion, while slicing some tough sausage, Ivona cut open the flesh between thumb and forefinger on her left hand, and while she was bent over in pain, Mario stood curiously to the side, wringing his hands together as was his habit. After a few moments, as she tried to wrap a cloth around her hand, he walked past her toward an empty juice container, one of his favourite toys, and sat down to play with it.

In the fall of 1990, after half a year of marriage, Ivona and

Sven simply locked up the little bachelor flat that had been the home of their married existence, and emigrated to Canada. Their decision happened swiftly, times were uncertain, Ivona was five months pregnant, and the opportunity was not to be had again. Despite cool family relations, Sven's uncle sponsored their emigration. After two years, Sven attempted to bring his parents over. Ivona didn't object, but most of her focus in those days was on her son, his unusual behaviour, and the doctor's tentative suggestion that he might have a condition called autism. It was another year before Ivona and Sven managed to work out a visiting visa for his parents. They arrived looking distraught and lost. Sven's mother was constantly on the verge of tears, and his father looked tiredly stoic. Initially the five of them—Mario was almost two years old then—lived together in Ivona and Sven's one-bedroom apartment. The parents slept in the bedroom, and Ivona and Sven and Mario on a mattress they had acquired secondhand and kept in the living-room until they were able to buy a couch or sofa. Sven's parents hadn't brought much, only one photo album, some clothes, and one particularly dear, and aged, ceramic tea set. "We thought we would be back in a few months," Sven's mother said repeatedly. She also said, on the second day of being in their apartment, "I thought you would have done better for yourselves." What she mostly meant was the lack of furniture. Ivona told her it was minimalism they were going for. "But where are people supposed to sit when they come over?" the mother asked. What she wanted as a sign of their success were heavy armchairs with carved wooden armrests, Oriental rugs, a wall-unit filled with crystal. "If I sit on the floor, my friends sit on the floor," Ivona replied. "What will become of you two here?" the mother wailed. "This is it," Ivona said. "What you see, is what we've become."

Both grandparents initially stressed how handsome Mario was, but after a little while they talked more and more about why he didn't even answer to his name, why he continually wriggled out of Grandma's lap. Insinuations of guilt hovered preciously above their words. After two weeks they went to spend a weekend at Sven's uncle's, his dad's brother's house. Sven and Ivona spent the weekend fighting over a missed appointment with the paediatrician. Sven slept alone on the mattress in the living-room. On Monday morning, the day Sven's parents were to return, Ivona woke in her marriage bed, a double bed with no bed frame, with her son's sleeping body next to her, his head at her hip. Her first thought was of her mother-in-law, the small-shouldered, black-haired figure, nestling into a corner of the living-room mattress, propped up by pillows, like a small animal, burrowing. Bringing crumbs of pastry up to her lips on fingers wet with saliva. And the father-in-law, calling over to Mario, "Come to Grandpa, little man," then throwing up his hands when Mario ignores him. Murmuring words to himself. These were her thoughts that morning, when she heard the front door unlocking.

They were in the hallway, the father struggling to get his coat off, the mother holding up a plastic bag and saying to Sven, "We had the best veal at your uncle's." Ivona emerged from the bedroom, and walked toward them saying, "You know what, I'm sorry, keep your coats on, you can't stay here." Sven couldn't have anticipated that she would go that far. He threw his arms out, glaring, disbelieving. "Have you gone crazy? Don't listen to her." He tried to move them inside, but his parents stood immobile, with long, blank faces. "No, no, you can't stay here, there is no room, go to your brother's house, he's rich, we're not rich." Neither of them spoke, Sven was clutching his head, and Ivona continued, "I'm not fucking around. If they stay"—she turned to her husband—"I will go." Now Sven's mother's eyes moistened and her chin trembled, and she dropped the plastic bag of veal leftovers she had been holding, while his father stood very still, as if he were standing on one piece of blessed solid ground amidst an earthquake. "I will go," Ivona said, "and I'll take my son, you goddam assholes."

Ivona has just finished a Friday closing shift. She is the last one in the restaurant, except for Will, who has stayed in his office for the last three hours instead of leaving at dinnertime, as he usually does. She knows of course that he's waiting for her to finish work. She can't avoid going to his office to hand over her cash. The door is open a crack, and as she enters she sees that he is sitting still, a calculator and a book open in front of him, but it doesn't look like he's touched either for hours. "Thank you," he says. At first she would just like to leave, but then she asks what he's doing here so late. "Kim's off somewhere, one of those Avon parties or something. So much freakin' paperwork to catch up on." He rubs his eyes. "Maybe we should have a drink, you and me, now that the place is empty. I've got keys to the bar, you know." He smiles. After a moment's silence, she says, "Do you want to take a ride, Will? Just a ride, we can talk for a bit." He looks uncertain and a little excited. "A ride?" "We'll take my car," she says.

It's cool in her old Subaru, the fall night is getting colder. They drive in silence, and she isn't sure where she's going, or why she's going anywhere at all. Something in Will annoys her to the point of intervention. The checkered shirts he wears, the way he sneaks up on her from behind to say "Hi." She is driving toward her own apartment, she realizes. Here is that Baptist church she passes by almost every day. She has no idea what a Baptist church might be like; she has only once back home heard of someone who went abroad and became a Baptist, or rather strayed into it. She turns into the parking-lot of the church.

"Well, this is an odd place to stop."

"I live close by here, I just didn't want to go any further."

"Ivona, Ivona. Is your husband up waiting for you?"

"He usually is."

"How old were you when you got married? You're 29

now, right?"

"I'm 30. I was 23. Had my son at 24."

"That's like me, I was even younger. Too freakin' young. Lots of things I haven't done, travel and stuff. I'd like to travel, go back to Belgium maybe, that's where my parents are from. All these girls working for me, they take vacations, go to Europe, go to—I don't know—Latin America, they're young, they can do whatever they want. Maybe I'll do all that stuff when I retire, I want to retire early, definitely. Right now, the way things are going, with the restaurant and everything, I could probably retire in ten years, if I don't lose it before then, my kids'll be grown, I'll ship them off to school somewhere, and just lie somewhere on a beach drinking those fruity drinks, whatever they are. But you need about a million to retire decently, you know, that's what I figure—"

"A million dollars? You need a million dollars to retire?"

"Well, I figure—What are you looking at me like that for? Hmm? Am I boring you, are you laughing at me? You're quite a beautiful lady, you know."

This dreamy look in his eyes, this fake dreamy look, fake husky voice, mockery of seduction. "He doesn't even really want me," she thinks.

"I'm not, obviously." She means beautiful. "Will, you should ask her, you should ask Kim, about all this retirement. You'll still be young in ten years."

They sit in silence for a little while, each looking out their own window.

"I feel like kissing you. Is that really bad? I shouldn't be saying these things to you, but I do want to, I do, I'm an honest guy, a simple guy."

The car has been on the whole time and now she shifts it into gear.

"I'm sorry, you're right, we should go home," he says.

She drives back to the restaurant. That's where his car is. If Sven knew this was going on, he would say, "You can quit, if it's a problem. We can do without the money." In front of the restaurant, as he's about to get out of the car, Will says, "I'm sorry. I'm out of line. Forgive me." His eyes have cleared from the haze of dreaminess.

"It's forgotten," she says.

After Ivona had sent her in-laws out of her apartment, she and Sven fought for days. "Do you know there is a war on? Would you have them go back to that, is that what you want?" She had never seen him so jerky with rage. Mario had several hysterical crying episodes in those few days. She read somewhere, later, that children with autism often suffer from inner anxiety. "You are such a hard woman," Sven said to her on the third day, when they were getting worn down. He said he might never forgive her, and in revenge she took back her forgiveness for everything she had ever held against him.

Now she drives back home, past the same Baptist church, and finds Sven sitting up in the kitchen with Mario, trying to get him to draw. Mario is puncturing the paper with the crayon, and Sven keeps saying "Easy, son." She sits down beside her husband. He is a dark-haired man, with a wide face. His skin is milky-pale, inherited by their son. There is a spot of black grease near Sven's temple, and a stray eyelash nestled near the bridge of his nose. Ivona, before she kisses them both, and touches both of their faces, can see all this clearly.

BARBARA ROMANIK is a graduate of the UNB Masters in English program but currently lives in Edmonton. Her fiction has appeared or is forthcoming in a number of periodicals including *Prism, Qwerty, Other Voices, Descant, Malahat* and *The Fiddlehead.*

J.M. VILLAVERDE lived in six countries in six years as a child, but has spent most of the last 30 years in Montreal, where he works as a marketing and business writer. He studied English, film and communications at McGill, while writing plays for amateur and student productions.

JASMINA ODOR was born and raised in Croatia, but moved to Canada with her family twelve years ago. She is currently working on an MA in comparative literature at the University of Alberta, while completing her first collection of stories.

MARK ANTHONY JARMAN is the author of *Salvage King Ya!, New Orleans is Sinking, 19 Knives and Ireland's Eye.* He has won the Gold Medal at the National Magazine Awards, and was a co-winner of the *Prism international* Short Fiction Contest. He is the fiction editor of *Fiddlehead* and teaches at UNB.

Previous volumes in this series contained stories by the following writers:

Most of these books are still available. Please inquire.